POLITICAL BOMBSHELL

Joe caught a glimpse of Frank standing near his chair, staring out into the darkness with a taut expression on his face.

"Frank! Over here!" Joe called. Frank turned toward his brother's voice as a white-orange flash lit the back of the stage like a burst of lightning.

Joe grabbed Callie and Vanessa and pulled them down. A deafening roar filled the auditorium. Bricks clattered down, and a cloud of acrid smoke and dust billowed out over the screaming crowd.

Joe jumped up and scanned the rubble-strewn stage. "Frank!" he called again. "Frank!"

His brother was nowhere in sight.

Books in THE HARDY BOYS CASEFILES™ Series

Available from ARCHWAY Paperbacks

THE HARDY BOYS CASEFILES NO. 103

CAMPAIGN OF CRIME

FRANKLIN W. DIXON

AN ARCHWAY PAPERBACK
Published by POCKET BOOKS
New York   London   Toronto   Sydney   Tokyo   Singapore

AN ARCHWAY PAPERBACK *Original*

An Archway Paperback published by
POCKET BOOKS, a division of Simon & Schuster Inc.
1230 Avenue of the Americas, New York, NY 10020

Copyright © 1995 by Simon & Schuster Inc.
Produced by Mega-Books, Inc.

ISBN: 0-671-88214-7

First Archway Paperback printing September 1995

10 9 8 7 6 5 4 3 2 1

THE HARDY BOYS, AN ARCHWAY PAPERBACK and colophon are registered trademarks of Simon & Schuster Inc.

THE HARDY BOYS CASEFILES is a trademark of Simon & Schuster Inc.

Cover art by Brian Kotzky

Printed in the U.S.A.

IL 6+

CAMPAIGN OF CRIME

Chapter

1

"I STILL DON'T BELIEVE THIS, JOE!" Vanessa Bender exclaimed.

Seventeen-year-old Joe Hardy grinned silently at his girlfriend. They were standing near the top of a low hill. To the north, the waters of Long Island Sound glistened in the sunlight. Along the shore was a huge concrete structure that looked like a giant grain silo.

Vanessa pointed an accusing finger at the building. "You brought us here to have a picnic? With a view of a nuclear power plant?" she continued.

Joe shrugged. "I didn't know it would bother you," he said easily. "I thought you knew about the Red Creek Reactor. It's perfectly safe—as long as nothing goes wrong."

Joe's older brother, Frank, and his girlfriend, Callie Shaw, were busy putting paper plates out on a blanket on the ground. Callie looked up and met Joe's eye. "You're such a comfort. Now we can all relax, right? We're perfectly safe— *as long as nothing goes wrong.*"

"Hey, guys, lighten up," Frank said. "The sun's shining, the birds are chirping, and Joe and I've got a two-hour vacation from worrying about the Webster for President campaign."

"Maybe you should make it a permanent vacation. I don't know why you're working for that yo-yo anyway," Callie teased. "Never mind—I do know. It got you off school for a week. Anyway, Josephine Montaldo's the better candidate."

Joe hunkered down at the edge of the blanket and reached for a bottle of mineral water. "Then how come you're hot to attend the Webster rally in Bayport tonight?" he asked. "Because he's rich and handsome?"

"Give me a break," Callie replied as she put a handful of chips and a sandwich on everyone's plate. "I want to see the guy sweat when I ask him why there are so few women executives in his computer company."

Joe finished two sandwiches before the others ate one. "Politics is hard work," he groaned. "First Frank signs on as Webster's youth coordinator for Bayport, then he ropes me into helping him. I'm just glad the primary's only two days away. Once it's over, maybe we can have fun again."

Vanessa rummaged around in a bag and produced a Frisbee. "Why not start now?" she asked, smiling. "Who wants to work off some of that terrific lunch?"

"Me," Joe yelled, grabbing the Frisbee and running with it. When he reached the top of the hill, he launched it toward his tall, brown-haired brother. Frank caught the whirling red disk behind his back.

The girls joined in, and the game took on a life of its own. It ended thirty minutes later when Frank and Joe dove for the Frisbee at once, with Frank squished under his burly younger brother. When the two of them got to their feet, Frank had the Frisbee and ran with it toward the van. "Sorry, guys," he said over his shoulder. "It's time to pack it in. I've got to check in at campaign headquarters to work on the rally."

After they loaded the van, the foursome got in, with Frank at the wheel. As he drove back to Bayport, Frank realized that he was getting more and more excited about the Webster rally. He'd read all of the computer genius's books, listened to his speeches, and even corresponded with him via E-mail, but now he was finally going to see him in person. Better yet, he, Joe,

Callie, and Vanessa were invited to a private meeting with Webster after the rally.

"Hey, Frank," Joe called from the backseat. "Wake up—our exit's coming up!"

Frank flipped the turn signal, slowed down, and edged onto the exit ramp. At the light he turned left, toward Callie's house. "How about we come back for you around seven?" he said as he pulled up in front. "That'll give us time to pick up Alex Davids."

Frank glanced over at Callie. He knew that she was taken with Davids. Most people who met him were. A forty-year-old man from Harlem who had gone to Harvard on scholarship, Davids was now the chair of the political science department at Bayport University. He had taken a leave of absence from the university to run Webster's primary campaign in the Northeast because he and Webster had been friends since college.

"I forgot Dr. Davids was coming with us," Callie replied, her face brightening. "That'll be great. Don't worry, I'll be ready on time."

Frank was late as he steered the van up the drive to the main entrance of Alex Davids's downtown condominium. Davids was waiting at the door, elegant in a light tan suit tailored to show off his trim, athletic body. A doorman in a blue uniform, with enough gold braid to outfit

4

a banana republic general, hurried over to slide open the side door of the van. Davids joined Callie and Vanessa in the backseat.

"Well," Davids said as they pulled away, "I just spoke to Nathan, and he's excited about meeting you."

"He's excited?" Frank exclaimed. "I've been wondering if I'll be able to calm down enough to get a single word out."

Davids chuckled. "I bet Callie doesn't feel that way," he said, lightly tapping her knee. "She'll probably call our distinguished candidate a techno-elitist and give him the same lecture on the virtues of old-fashioned grass roots politics that she gave me the other day."

Frank glanced in the rearview mirror at Callie. She was blushing.

"Not at all," she said. "I may ask difficult questions, but I'll certainly be polite."

"You've got to admit that Webster *is* a remarkable guy," Frank said to Callie. "A computer whiz whose business ideas could change the face of the country."

"True," Callie admitted. "It's just that I'm not sure he's qualified to be president of the United States."

On the corner of Fourth Street the old, ornate facade of the Bayport Auditorium came into view. Built in the thirties, the building had been a movie theater until ten years ago. Frank could remember going there as a young kid. He wasn't sure he liked the way the inside had been gutted and made over into a sparse modern hall, but at least it hadn't been torn down. Because of the auditorium this part of town was making a comeback after having become pretty run-down.

The entrance to the staff parking lot was on the far side of the building. As Frank slowed down to turn into it, he saw that some anti-Webster demonstrators had set up a picket line in front of the auditorium.

Vanessa read a couple of the picketers' signs aloud. " 'Ban Computer Politics.' What do you suppose that means? 'Save Mother Earth—Unplug Webster.' "

Davids laughed. "More technology haters. I guess what they're saying is that they don't want the information superhighway to run through their backyards."

"Do they expect information to travel on horseback, like in the days of the pony express?" asked Joe.

"Could be," Davids answered.

"Well," said Callie, "I wouldn't go that far, but I like the one about Big Brother."

"I'm not surprised," Frank said. "But listen, Callie, will you at least keep an open mind during the interactive experiment tonight?" That was the part of the program that really had Frank intrigued. Everyone in the audience was going to have access to a laptop computer. They would all be hooked up to one another by a fiber-optic network. Webster would organize the interactions, but in theory, by the end of the evening, the audience would be speaking for itself, just as Nathan Webster wanted everyone in the country to be able to do.

"I'm open-minded," Callie replied. "But that doesn't mean I'm going to give up my opinions."

After Frank pulled into the last reserved parking spot, they all got out. At the stage door they showed their passes and went inside.

"We're just in time," Joe said as he paused to scan the scene. The curtains that usually hid the backstage area had been taken down. The lights, equipment, and banks of computers were in full view of the audience. Even the stage door itself was in plain sight. "Pretty cool," Joe commented. "It's like saying, 'I've got nothing to hide, folks.' "

"Quite a crowd," Callie commented, surveying the full auditorium.

"Oh, look—there's Nathan," Alex Davids pointed out. "Still fiddling with the computers, of course."

Joe looked. The presidential hopeful was bent over a computer, examining the wiring. His black turtleneck, faded jeans, and loafers made him look like a college student, except for his longish black hair, which was streaked with gray. When he straightened up, Joe was struck by his high forehead and determined jaw.

Alex Davids fingered his patterned blue silk tie. "Success hasn't changed Nathan a bit," he said dryly. "Not even his wardrobe."

Webster glanced across the stage and gave someone a thumbs-up sign. The houselights blinked twice, then twice again, signaling that the program was about to begin.

"We'd better get to our seats," Davids said. "Callie, Vanessa, Joe—I reserved places for you in the front row. Frank and I have to be up onstage with the candidate."

Joe grinned and punched Frank in the arm. "Enjoy your five minutes of fame," he teased. "But just remember, if you blow it everyone will be watching."

The three teens made their way down the stairs to their seats, which had been fitted with flip-up desks. On top of each one was a laptop computer.

The three of them had just settled in when the houselights dimmed. Minutes later the candidate, Dr. Davids, Frank, and a number of other dignified-looking people took seats on the stage. Davids rose to make a brief introduction, then turned the microphone over to Webster.

When Webster began to speak, Joe found himself wondering why the guy was running for office. He was obviously very bright and full of ideas, but he wasn't a dynamic speaker—until he started getting the audience ready to interact on-line. As the spectators turned on their computers, they all seemed to catch Webster's enthusiasm.

Joe scanned the menu on the first screen, then used the trackball to cursor down and check off Age 15-18 and Student. He was moving the cursor to the category Where I Live when the screen went dead.

At that same moment the sound system went out. Webster tapped his forefinger on the mike, then held up a hand as if to say, "Wait a minute." Turning, he walked across the stage to one of the clusters of computers.

Callie turned to Joe and whispered, "Not a very high-tech operation."

Joe shrugged. "Maybe somebody forgot to pay the electricity bill," he joked. "If that's—"

Suddenly every light in the auditorium went out. There were scattered screams. From onstage, somebody shouted, "Take it easy. It's a minor problem. We'll have it fixed in a jiffy."

Joe wasn't so sure of that. An overloaded circuit could have caused the regular lighting to fail, but why had the emergency lights gone out, too? Each of those lights had its own battery-powered pack. When the electricity failed the batteries should have kicked in automatically. He fumbled in his jacket pocket for his penlight.

As minutes passed and the auditorium remained pitch-black, the crowd grew more and more uneasy. Onstage, half a dozen powerful flashlights were converging on one spot. Joe assumed that they belonged to security guards, closing in to protect the candidate. They formed a tight circle that began to move toward the stage door.

"Joe, what is it? What's happening?" Vanessa demanded.

"I think the guards are taking Webster out of the building to protect him," Joe replied in an undertone. "Come on—let's join Frank on the stage. That way we'll all be together."

He grabbed Callie's arm and used his penlight to guide the girls along the railing separating the audience from the orchestra pit to the stairs leading onto the stage. Joe was just about there when he caught a glimpse of Frank standing near his chair, his face lit by a flashlight. He was staring out into the darkness with a taut expression on his face.

"Frank! Over here!" Joe called. Frank turned toward his brother's voice as a white-orange flash lit the back of the stage like a burst of lightning. Joe grabbed Callie and Vanessa and pulled them down. A deafening roar filled the auditorium. Bricks clattered down, and a cloud of acrid smoke and dust billowed out over the screaming crowd.

Joe jumped up and scanned the rubble-strewn stage, now partially lit from a gaping hole in the back wall. "Frank!" he called again. "Frank!"

His brother was nowhere in sight.

Chapter

2

DAZED, FRANK PUSHED HIMSELF UP into a sitting position. His head was pounding, and his lungs ached from the thick dust he had breathed in. What had happened? He tried to think. He had turned to the edge of the stage to help Joe and the girls up. But then what? Had he fallen over the edge in the dark? That didn't sound right. . . .

Just then he remembered the flash, roar, and shock wave that had knocked him to the floor. What had it done to Davids? Frank tried to shout his name, but he couldn't hear himself over the screaming in the auditorium. He crawled forward through the dusty air toward where he thought Davids had been. He found him and accidentally touched Davids's shoulder. It was wet—with blood.

Davids drew in a sharp breath, then gasped, "Frank?"

"Yes. Don't move," Frank replied. "I'll try to get help."

"Don't bother, I'm okay," Davids said weakly. "But Nathan . . ."

Frank looked over his shoulder, in the direction of the stage door. The door wasn't there anymore, and neither was most of the wall around it. From the parking lot, bright light streamed in through the ragged opening. Where it shone he could see only rubble and a few larger forms he was afraid were people. If Nathan Webster had been anywhere near that back wall, he might not have survived.

"What was it?" Davids continued. "A bomb?"

"Seems like it," Frank replied. "We'd better—"

He didn't finish the sentence. From the auditorium came a crash, then the screaming grew louder and more hysterical. Frank ran toward the edge of the stage, shining a light down onto the crowd. The railing between the audience and the orchestra pit had given way under the weight of the surging crowd. Those closest to it had been hurled into the six-and-a-half-foot pit.

Now others were falling in on top of them, pushed from behind.

"Frank? Is that you?" came a familiar voice.

"Joe, you're okay!" Frank grabbed Joe's arm. "What about Callie and Vanessa?"

"We're okay," Callie assured him. "We climbed up the stairs before everyone got hysterical."

"We've got to do something, quick," Frank said. "Otherwise somebody's going to get crushed to death!"

"But what, Frank?" Joe demanded. He panned the audience with his light. "Look, the doors to the lobby are blocked with people. That's why the others are all pushing down to the front. This is a nightmare."

"We've got to figure out some way to get the crowd to back off," Frank said.

"I know. Maybe we can get some of them to move out the emergency side exits," Joe replied. "I'll be right back."

He ran off into the wings on the left side of the stage. Vanessa started to follow, but Frank stopped her.

"Let him go, Vanessa," Frank said. "He can handle himself better alone. Anyway, I thought I saw something we can use. Come on." He led the way toward a hole in the wall where several people were stumbling out. Close to the hole he found what he had seen from a distance. Scattered across the stage floor were half a dozen big, powerful flashlights that must have been dropped by the security guards. Why, he didn't know. He picked one up and turned it on, sending a tight beam of white light across the backstage area.

"Great," he said to Vanessa and Callie. "Now, listen—gather up three flashlights each, then point them up to the balcony into the spotlight. I'm going to look for Alex Davids and Nathan Webster."

"I get it!" Vanessa exclaimed. "The large metal dish around the spotlight will reflect the light out for people to see by. Come on, Callie. Let's do it."

Frank looked around and was glad that most of the people backstage seemed to be merely stunned. The bomb must have been on the outside of the stage door, primed to explode when the guards swung the door open. Maybe the heavy metal door had deflected the main force of the blast and shielded the people nearest to the bomb from most of the flying debris. Frank didn't like to think about what happened to the person who opened the door.

"Frank. Quick, over here!" Alex Davids was bending down next to someone on the floor beside the opening.

Frank headed to Davids's side.

"It's Nathan," Alex continued. "He's unconscious, but he's got a pulse. He must have been hit pretty hard on the head."

Frank knelt down and felt Webster's pulse. "It's weak," he said. Glancing around, he saw the bodies of three security guards lying face-down near the bent and charred remains of the stage door.

Davids shook his head. "All dead, I'm afraid," he said. "One of them must have opened the door and caught the full force of the blast. He saved Nathan's life."

"*If* the EMS guys get here soon enough," Frank said. As he got to his feet he glanced out into the night. The staff parking lot was eerily quiet, in stark contrast to the scene of horror behind him.

A soot-covered security guard was leaning against the wall, speaking into his walkie-talkie. Frank overheard him say, "Dead and injured. Send every ambulance you can, and *fast.*"

Other survivors were sitting on the pavement outside, too stunned to move. Where were the emergency vehicles? What was taking them so long? Then Frank realized that only minutes had passed since the blast. It seemed like a lifetime.

Somewhere in the distance, sirens wailed. Overhead, the *whup-whup-whup* of a helicopter drew closer. Help was on the way.

Frank was turning to go back to help when,

out of the corner of his eye, he noticed something moving. An old red pickup with rounded front fenders was driving slowly toward the parking lot exit. Frank frowned. Why would someone be driving away at a time like this?

As he took a step forward to get a closer look at the truck and its driver, a police car came skidding around the corner. Its lights were flashing and its siren screaming. Instantly the red pickup peeled away. Alerted, Frank dashed outside, jumped off the stairs, and ran toward the street, hoping to catch a glimpse of the license plate. Too late—the truck was already vanishing around the corner with its lights out.

Just then three EMS vans careened into the parking lot. Frank stood aside as the teams of medics rushed past him into the building. Then he followed. Two of them were examining Webster and treating his injuries when Frank got back onstage. Davids beckoned Frank to join him.

"I think they made it in time for Nathan," Davids said.

"So do I," Frank replied. Then he told Davids about the pickup truck. "It may not mean anything, but remind me to mention it to the police. Maybe it's not too late to pick up the driver."

Davids nodded grimly. "I certainly will."

Frank looked past Davids toward the stage opening. He could see Callie and Vanessa aiming their flashlights at the spotlight on the balcony. The feeling of panic had lessened in the auditorium as people were managing to find their way out.

"I'm going to see if I can help," Frank said, nodding toward the auditorium. "I'll catch up with you later at the hospital."

Frank crossed the stage to where Callie was standing.

"Your idea seems to be working," she said, motioning with her head out into the dimly lit hall. "Joe opened some side exits, but a lot of the people in the crowd are still spooked and unable to move."

Vanessa, who had been standing nearer to the lip of the stage, hurried over. Her blond hair was darkened by the soot that still hung in the air. "Frank, we've got to get all of those people out of the pit—now."

Joe rejoined them in time to hear her. "I managed to force my way through the crowds to open three exit doors on the side of the building," he said. "Once people saw the lights from outside, they headed for them. It's taken off some of the pressure on the main lobby."

"I'm glad you're okay. I was pretty scared," Vanessa said, her eyes shining.

"So was I," Joe admitted. Through the huge hole in the wall, he could see that the parking lot was filling up with emergency vehicles. Uniformed rescue workers were filtering onto the stage. A three-person television news crew was already inside and starting to film.

"Hey, Frank," Joe yelled. "Give me a hand."

"You got it," Frank replied, following his brother to the edge of the stage.

Joe lay down on his stomach and began to creep forward until his head and shoulders hung down into the orchestra pit. "Hold my legs," he told Frank. "I'll pull people up."

Frank clasped his brother's ankles firmly. Joe reached down. A moment later he felt as if he had stumbled into a scene from a horror movie. Hands clutched at his arms and tugged at him, accidentally pulling him down into the pit. He felt himself slipping forward, until the edge of the stage was digging into his waist. Worse, Frank was being pulled forward, too. If they didn't do something right away, both of them were going to tumble headfirst into the orchestra pit.

"Pull me back, Frank!" Joe shouted desperately. "Back!" He shook his arms while Frank tugged on his legs. Finally he rolled onto the stage and lay on his back to catch his breath.

Vanessa rushed over. "Joe? Are you okay?" she demanded.

He nodded wordlessly.

"I'm going to try to help from the auditorium," Frank said. "You stay here and wait for help."

As Frank dashed off, a firefighter moved onstage, carrying a portable floodlight. He switched it on and pointed it into the auditorium. A moment later another light came on. Joe saw Frank at the far end of the stage as he ran down the steps and stepped onto the floor of the auditorium beside the pit.

"Oh, no!" Joe gasped. Now that the hall was lit again, the crowd could see where the stairs to the stage were. With no thought but escape, they pushed toward them. Frank was standing directly in front of the stairs, blocking their way.

"Frank, look out!" Callie yelled. Too late. In that instant Frank was knocked down. He vanished.

Chapter
3

JOE PUSHED THROUGH THE CROWD on the stage. He sensed that Callie and Vanessa were close behind. As he moved, Joe tried to analyze the situation as coolly as possible and weigh all his options.

Did they have any? He wasn't sure. Lines of people were still funneling toward the stairs, desperate to get out of the auditorium. What was Joe going to do, ask them to let him pass? Try to elbow his way through? Either way, he wouldn't get anywhere at all—or else he, too, would be knocked down. That wouldn't help Frank.

As Joe ran toward the side of the stage, he noticed a door leading off it to the dressing

21

rooms backstage. Maybe it would provide a way back into the auditorium without forcing him to elbow his way through the crowd.

He dashed over to it, twisted the knob, and pushed. The door flew open suddenly, dumping him on the floor. He picked himself up. Beyond the open doorway was a short down staircase with a closed door at the bottom.

Joe took the five steps at one leap and shoved the door with his shoulder. It flew open into a narrow hall, revealing the surprised face of a young police officer. The officer jerked his nightstick up in both hands, holding it chest-high, as if ready to push Joe back.

"Does that door lead back into the auditorium?" Joe asked, pointing straight ahead.

"Yeah," the officer replied. "But you can't go through there."

"I've got to," Joe told him. "My brother was knocked down in there beside the stage. He may be badly hurt. I've got to get to him!"

"Listen, friend, it's a madhouse through that door," the officer said. "We're trying to clear the hall in case there's another bomb set to go off."

"But, Officer," Joe said, "my brother should be right through that door. We'll just get him and get out—I promise."

The officer frowned, then gave a quick nod. "Well, okay," he said.

Joe motioned toward the door with his head, then he, Vanessa, and Callie hurried through. In the aisle ahead of them a steady stream of people flowed past on their way outside. Joe and the girls hugged the wall of the auditorium, looking in the direction they'd last seen Frank.

Where could he be? Joe knew that his brother had either regained his footing and been pushed along with the crowd, or he'd been knocked to the floor. In that case, he'd be somewhere up ahead and almost certainly in bad shape. As he stood waiting for a break in the flow of people, Joe kept searching for Frank among the people moving slowly by. Several times he thought he saw Frank's brown hair or his blue shirt, only to be disappointed.

Once the audience members finally made it to the door outside, they calmed down—and terror gave way to despair. In the harsh glare of the whirring emergency lights, their faces appeared drawn and sickly.

Joe began calling Frank's name as he searched, moving along the wall. Behind him, Vanessa and Callie were also shouting.

"Oh, no!" Joe said under his breath. Just ahead, lying next to the wall, was someone. Frank.

Joe rushed over and knelt down. His brother was unconscious, but there were no obvious marks or cuts on him. Joe pressed a hand to the side of his brother's neck and felt a faint pulse.

"Joe!" Callie cried. "Is he—"

"Vanessa, see if you can get the medics," Joe said. "And make it fast."

He tilted Frank's head back and cradled it in his arms, hoping to see a light of recognition flash in his brother's eyes. But they remained glazed and unseeing.

"This way, quick!" Joe heard Vanessa shout.

He looked up. An EMS team was making its way through the crowd, burdened with a medical kit, oxygen tank, and folding stretcher. One of the medics knelt down beside Frank and did a quick evaluation, then looked up and gave Joe a short nod. "We'll take it from here."

Joe got to his feet and took a step back. Callie was standing there, gazing down at Frank, with an expression of shock and terror. Joe put his arm around her shoulders and said, "Don't worry. He'll be okay."

"Are you sure?" Callie begged, her voice trembling.

"Of course I am," Joe said. He put every ounce of confidence he had left into his voice. Still, his words rang hollow.

The team of medics put a brace around Frank's neck, strapped him to a long board, and slid him onto the stretcher. As Joe followed them toward the exit, Vanessa took his hand and squeezed it.

The medic nearest him was a short, stocky woman who seemed to be in charge of the team.

"He's my brother, Frank," Joe told her. "Will he be okay?"

The woman have him a sympathetic look. "There's really nothing I can tell you right now," she replied. "He had no wounds, but head trauma is what the doctors will deal with."

They moved down a side alley toward Fourth Street, where the ambulance was waiting. By now the crowd had thinned, and most of the people around were medics, going back and forth to load the injured into ambulances. Surprisingly, very few of the people who had fallen into the orchestra pit had sustained any serious injuries.

Fourth Street was still filled with people who had been at the rally, unable to tear themselves away. The police were gently prodding them to move along to make way for the EMS, but it was only with difficulty that the medics wove through the crowd, carrying Frank's stretcher.

Joe looked closely at Frank one last time as they put him in the ambulance. "Is it a good sign that he's not bleeding?" Joe asked.

"Could be," the woman said in a neutral tone. "Excuse me." She swung the ambulance door closed.

Joe swallowed the lump in his throat. "Where are you taking him?" he asked.

"St. Vincent's," she told him. "They're setting

up a special trauma center there for the victims."

Then the ambulance pulled away, its roof lights flashing. As he turned to go back to the parking lot, Joe noticed a pay phone on the corner. "Duty calls," he muttered to Vanessa. "But I'm not looking forward to this."

He dialed his home number. His mother answered on the first ring. "Hi, Mom," Joe said. He was more choked up than he'd realized, and his voice came out quavery.

"Joe, are you all right?" Laura Hardy demanded. "I've been worried to death. Callie's mother called when she heard about the explosion on the news."

"No, I'm fine," Joe said. "But . . . well, Frank was knocked out. They just took him to St. Vincent's. They don't know how bad it is yet."

His mother took in a quick breath, then said, "I'll be right there."

"I'll see you at the hospital," Joe replied. "And, Mom—don't worry. He'll be okay."

Joe hung up and turned to Callie and Vanessa. "Your parents heard about the bomb blast on the news," he said. "You'd better call them and let them know you're not hurt."

Callie was pale. "My mom will want to hear about Frank, too. I wish I knew what to tell her."

Joe peered over her shoulder, up the alley.

Two medics were loading another stretcher into an ambulance. There was a sheet covering the face of that victim.

"Tell her Frank's alive," Joe said, his voice trembling. "That's all we can say right now."

An hour later Joe, his mother, Callie, and Vanessa were gathered in one corner of the hospital cafeteria. The big room had been set aside as a place for relatives of victims to wait for news.

"You'd think they could tell us *something* specific," Joe muttered to Vanessa.

"Look around," Vanessa replied in a low voice. "There are a couple hundred people here, and they're all in the same boat. The doctors and nurses are too busy dealing with patients to worry about us. Oh, look—the news is coming on. Let's go watch."

A crowd gathered in front of the big TV in the corner of the room. Joe and the girls joined it, though Joe was not really that interested. He knew the police wouldn't have released any leads this early, and he already knew all too well the tally of victims: over a hundred with minor breaks and bruises, thirty in serious condition, ten critical, and four deaths. Trampling injuries had turned out to be more numerous and just as serious as those inflicted by the blast.

Only half listening, Joe suddenly heard the

27

news announcer say, "And this just in. Earlier today, the *New York Post* received a communiqué from a group calling itself the Green Warriors. In it, this previously unknown group threatened to, and I quote, 'unplug' Nathan Webster's presidential campaign. Immediately after the Bayport explosion, someone claiming to speak for the Green Warriors called the *Post* to claim responsibility for the attack. The caller also threatened to act again if Webster didn't drop out of the race. Police officials refused to comment, but it is believed that they are on the trail of this terrorist group."

Joe turned to Callie and Vanessa. "Weird," he said. "I guess the 'green' in the name is supposed to mean they're pro-environment. Too bad they didn't explain how killing four people and terrorizing hundreds of others would help their cause."

Before he could continue, a bearded man in a nurse's uniform approached. "Laura Hardy?" he called, scanning the crowd.

"Here I am," Mrs. Hardy said.

Joe went to her side. With his father away on business, and his aunt Gertrude visiting friends, Joe knew his mother could use the support.

The nurse came over to them. "I'd like to speak to you about your son, Frank. A doctor usually does this, but we can spare no one now. I hope you'll understand. I have spoken to his doctor, of course. The good news is that Frank doesn't have a fractured skull—"

"And?" interrupted Laura. "Is there bad news, too?"

The man hesitated. "Well, maybe not. He is still unconscious, but that isn't too unusual. Sometimes it takes a while. But the doctors are watching him closely to make sure he doesn't develop an intracranial hematoma."

"I'm sorry," Laura said, biting her lip. "I'm not familiar with . . ."

"That means bleeding between the brain and the skull," the man explained. "If a clot forms, it could lead to serious problems. But this all takes time to diagnose."

"But Frank *is* okay now?" Callie asked hopefully.

The nurse hesitated again. "He could snap out of it at any time. But meanwhile, as a precaution, Dr. Burt has decided to put him on the critical list."

Chapter

4

CALLIE'S EYES WIDENED IN SHOCK. "The critical list!" she cried. "You mean Frank might not make it?"

Laura Hardy's face blanched. Joe put his arm around her, swallowed hard, and asked, "Where is he? Can we see him?"

The nurse gave him a sympathetic nod. "Sure," he said. "He's been moved to the neurosurgery ward—just as a precaution. Fourth floor, west wing."

"Thanks. Mom—"

Joe's question was interrupted by a man of about forty, wearing an expensive-looking but wrinkled dark brown suit. "Joe Hardy?" he asked.

Joe nodded in surprise. "That's right."

The man flashed a badge too quickly for Joe to read and added, "Ramon Diaz, FBI. I'm the chief field agent for the area. I'd like a word with you."

"Nice to meet you, Mr. Diaz," Joe said. "But I'm afraid this isn't a very good time. We were about to visit my brother, who's just been put on the critical list."

"I know," the agent said crisply. His dark eyes were cold as steel, and it was clear he wasn't going to back off. "We can talk on the way to the floor."

"Okay," Joe said reluctantly. He took his mother's arm and started toward the bank of elevators with Callie and Vanessa close behind.

Diaz asked, "What did your brother tell you about the truck he saw shortly after the explosion?"

"Why . . . nothing," Joe replied. "This is the first I heard of it. How do you know about it?"

"He told Professor Davids about it, and Davids told the police," Diaz said. "But the description was pretty vague."

He reached into his pocket. "Here's my card. Call me if Frank comes to and remembers anything."

Joe took the card, wincing a little at the way Diaz had said "if." "Yeah, I'll do that."

"One other thing, Joe," Diaz said, as the little

31

group stopped in front of the elevators. "Don't even think about trying to solve this case. I know you and your brother have done some good work in the past. But a lot may hang in the balance here. We can't afford to let amateurs foul up our investigation. Is that clear?"

Ordinarily, Joe would have bristled at this warning, but all he could think of now was seeing Frank. "Yes, sir," he said, as the elevator doors slid open.

Diaz turned and walked away. On the fourth floor, Laura Hardy was the first off the elevator. She hurried over to the nurses' station to ask where Frank was. When she turned back, Joe saw that though her eyes were damp, she was smiling. Joe took a deep breath. He could feel his shoulders start to relax.

"Frank has regained consciousness," Mrs. Hardy announced. She turned and hurried down the corridor with Joe and the girls on her heels.

When they reached the room, they found Frank playing with the controls on his bed. He looked up with a guilty grin. "They told me to lie flat," he said. "But it makes my headache worse."

"Frank, please do what they say," Laura chided. "You must have been hit pretty hard, you know."

Frank shook his head, then winced and groaned. "No, I *don't* know," he said. "And it's

32

driving me crazy. The last thing I remember before I woke up in this bed was the lights going out, then a big bang. What happened, anyway?"

Joe was starting to fill in the gaps in Frank's memory when someone tapped on the door. It was Alex Davids, his arm in a sling and his pants bloodstained. His jacket was slung over his shoulder.

"Frank, my man, you're awake!" he said, with a warm smile. "How do you feel?"

"A little rocky," Frank admitted. "How about you? And Webster? Is he okay?"

"I just came from him," Alex replied. "He's got a broken arm, some cuts and bruises, and his face looks like he lost in a back alley brawl. But his spirits are good. We were trying to sort out what happened and what it means."

Joe said, "You heard about the Green Warriors, then."

"Yes, of course," Alex replied. "Nathan was told about their threat this afternoon. He didn't take it seriously, though. Even when the power went off at the rally, he still didn't think of sabotage."

"Hey, slow down, guys," Frank said, working the controls to raise the back of his bed still higher. "Don't forget, all this is news to me."

Joe told him about the Green Warriors.

Frank scowled. "What kind of sense does that make?" he demanded. "Webster's got the backing of most of the major environmental groups. His computer plant is the cleanest in the industry."

"The major groups, maybe," Joe said. "But now we're talking crazies. Nobody who's playing with a full deck would set off a bomb at a political rally, where hundreds of people might be hurt."

Frank gazed off into space. "Anybody can make up a name," he said. "This Green Warriors business could easily be a smoke screen. What if the bombers *want* the authorities to waste their time checking out the big, militant, pro-environment groups?"

Alex smiled faintly. "I told Nathan that you fellows would be onto this the moment Frank came to," he said. "And he wasn't a bit disturbed to hear it."

Laura Hardy broke in. "Well, Dr. Davids," she said, "this is one investigation that Frank and Joe will have to discuss from the sidelines. That FBI agent seemed very efficient, didn't he, Joe?"

"What FBI agent?" Frank asked.

"A guy named Diaz," Joe told him. "He wanted to know if you'd told me anything about some truck you saw. I said no, then he warned me not to butt into his territory. End of conversation."

"Really?" Davids said. "I was thinking of

pulling you fellows off the campaign so you could investigate some local angles—quietly, of course."

"Against the express wishes of the FBI?" Laura said. "I certainly hope not! Besides, Frank is in no shape to do anything for the next several days."

"I wasn't suggesting that Frank leap out of bed to pursue the terrorists," Alex said smoothly. "But he can still use his mind, and he has Joe to do the legwork. I know Nathan would go for it. He's not convinced that the bomb was the work of one of the big environmental groups, either—even though the FBI believes it."

"So Frank's the brains and I'm the brawn, huh?" Joe said, pretending to be offended. "Thanks a lot!"

Alex grinned at him, then his face became somber. "Mrs. Hardy," he said, "when terrorists attack a political campaign, they're declaring war on our entire democratic system. They have to be stopped. And I think your sons have a very important contribution to make to that effort."

Joe could see the conflict and worry written on his mother's face. He understood. After all, Fenton Hardy, Joe and Frank's father, had spent many years in the New York Police Department before retiring to become an internationally known private detective. How many times had Laura Hardy watched him go off on an assignment, not knowing if he'd come back alive?

Before Laura could express her doubts, a portly, silver-haired man in a white coat walked in. He scanned Frank's chart, then gave him a quick but thorough examination.

"Ha!" he said, straightening up. "We'll have to get this young fellow off my ward. He's taking up precious space."

"You mean he's all right?" Joe demanded.

"He will be." The doctor turned to Laura. "Are you his mother? This looks like a minor concussion. We'll release him in the morning. But keep a close eye on him. If he develops nausea or if his pupils become unequal in size bring him right back in. Now I recommend that you all get some sleep."

The doctor left as fast as he had come in. Joe turned to his mother. "Don't worry, Mom," he assured her. "We'll just stick to sorting out the facts. No dangerous stuff, not after what we've just been through."

Joe could tell that she appreciated being humored, even if she didn't believe him for a second.

Frank began to fidget and act distracted. "Are you feeling all right?" Callie asked him. She and

Vanessa had been quietly keeping an eye on him from either side of the bed.

"I've been trying to remember anything about a truck," Frank said, sounding almost angry. "But it's not working. I think I remember staring out at the parking lot, but that's as far as I get."

"Don't worry about it, Frank," Callie said. "Just concentrate on getting some rest. You'll feel different in the morning." She took the controls and lowered the bed, then everyone said goodbye and filed out.

In the hallway Joe turned to Alex and asked, "Do you need a ride home?"

"Why, thank you, Joe." He looked at his watch and sighed. "I've got a campaign meeting first thing tomorrow morning."

"Why don't I take the girls home?" Laura asked.

Joe agreed and then went with Alex to retrieve the van from the visitors' parking lot. The streets of Bayport were almost deserted and it was raining lightly. Joe rolled down his window to sniff the fresh air outside. In the rearview mirror, he could just make out a pair of headlights glowing out from halos of mist.

Davids broke the silence. "I worry about what may happen next. These people clearly mean business, whoever they are."

"Yeah," replied Joe, stealing another glance

in the rearview mirror. The rain had stopped, and the mist was lifting. "They seem to know what they're doing. To cut the power *and* disarm the emergency lights while the whole audience was watching—well, that's pretty impressive."

"Impressive and frightening," Alex agreed. "And not knowing who we're dealing with makes it that much worse."

"That's probably just the effect they're after," Joe said. "Do you know if Webster has any enemies outside of political ones? A competitor in the computer business, maybe?"

"Anything's possible," Alex said slowly. "We're talking about a very tough business, after all. When Nathan developed that famous chip of his, it put quite a few people out of business."

Joe checked his mirror again. "What did Frank say to you about that truck he saw?" he asked.

If Alex was surprised by the sudden change of subject, he didn't show it. "Just that it was an old red truck with rounded fenders. Why?"

Joe nodded grimly. "We've got an old red truck on our tail. I don't want to tip them off that we've spotted them, but I don't think I'd better stop at your apartment building."

"I see your point," Alex said. "But where can we go that's safe?"

"I'll head for the police station on Ninth," Joe explained. "I can drive straight into the garage there."

Joe continued straight past Alex's condo, then turned left at the next corner. The truck was pulling up close behind them. The driver put his hand out the window.

"Hold on!" Joe shouted. He spun the wheel right and floored the accelerator. The van started to skid on the slick pavement. Joe steered out of the skid and was beginning to get the van under control when three closely spaced shots rang out.

The van lurched, then spun around. Joe and Alex ducked as two more gunshots broke the silence of the night.

Chapter
5

JOE HELD ON TO THE WHEEL tightly as the van hit the curb, bounced wildly, and slammed hard into something just behind his door. Still crouching down, he waited for more shots. Instead, he heard the growl of a powerful engine and the screech of the truck tires. As the sounds faded, he cautiously sat up and looked around.

Just down the block, a silver sedan had stopped and was now backing up and turning around. Joe didn't blame the driver. Why drive straight into a battle zone?"

"Are you okay, Professor Davids?" Joe asked.

Davids sat up, felt his bandaged arm, and said, "I'm fine, Joe. And, please, from now on call me Alex."

"You've got it," Joe told him. He reached for the cellular phone, dialed 911, and told the dispatcher what had happened. The truck was most likely far away by now, but the police might get lucky. Then he got out to inspect the damage to the van.

"Oh, rats!" he said to Alex. "One blowout and a nice big dent where we hit the streetlight. Did you spot a license plate?"

Alex laughed. "I was too busy dodging bullets," he admitted. "But I did get the impression there was only one person in the truck."

Joe opened the rear door of the van and took out the jack and the lug wrench. "That could explain why he was shooting off target," he said. "He was trying to drive at the same time."

"Not very efficient, to give one guy so much to do," Alex pointed out.

"Maybe he came after us on his own," Joe suggested as he pulled out the spare tire. "Though he must have been waiting for us at the hospital. I have a hunch he was after you, Alex. And if I'm right, he knows where you live. It was when I drove past your building that he moved in to attack. Do you think you ought to find someplace else to stay tonight?"

Alex thought for a few moments before saying, "My building's got good security, Joe. If I'm not safe there, I don't know where I would be.

"Besides," he added after a short silence. "I

41

can't imagine that I'm a primary target. They're probably just trying to shake up Webster by going after people on his team. Let's face it, Joe, we're just pawns in this game—whatever it is."

"Yeah—and we almost got sacrificed," Joe muttered under his breath.

By the time Joe changed the tire, dropped Alex by his building, and drove home, it was after midnight. To his amazement, there was a message from Frank on the answering machine.

"Listen, Joe," Frank's voice said. "I think we should go look for whatever shorted out the power as soon as possible, before some janitor sweeps the evidence away. Pick me up at five tomorrow morning at the hospital. Oh, and bring along Phil Cohen."

Phil, one of Bayport High's top science students, often helped the Hardys with the technical side of their investigations. Bringing him along made sense—though the five A.M. part did not. Joe went to bed wondering if Frank was a little delirious. The only way to find out would be to do as his brother suggested.

It felt like only minutes later when the alarm sounded in Joe's ear. He pulled on clothes, stumbled downstairs, and grabbed a carton of milk and a box of doughnuts on his way out to the van.

When he reached Phil's house, Joe threw pebbles at his friend's window. Nothing happened. Joe was tempted to heave a stone, but that would rouse the whole house, if not the whole neighborhood. Joe retreated to the van, plugged a high-candlepower spotlight into the lighter, and aimed it at the window, flooding Phil's room with light. After a few seconds, Phil was leaning out the window, staring like a startled owl.

"Phil, it's me, Joe," Joe called softly. "Come on down. I need your help."

"Can't it wait till morning?" Phil called back.

"No, I guess not, or you wouldn't be here."

He vanished from the window. Five minutes later he reappeared around the corner of the house, pulling a sweatshirt over his tousled hair.

"This wouldn't have something to do with that bombing last night, would it?" he asked when he reached the van.

"You win first prize," Joe replied. "A doughnut and some milk."

On the drive to the hospital, Joe told Phil about the events of the previous evening.

"Hmm," Phil said when Joe finished. "You expect to find some kind of timing device that killed the power."

"That's about it," Joe replied. "But don't

look at me. This was Frank's idea—and there he is."

Frank was standing to one side of the main entrance, dressed in his wrinkled clothes from the night before. He hurried over as Joe pulled up and then climbed into the back.

"What happened to the van?" he asked as they headed away from the hospital.

"The red truck was waiting for me and Alex Davids last night," Joe replied, and described what had happened.

Phil looked over at him. "Are you sure it's a good idea to return to the auditorium?" he asked. "What if that guy's waiting for us?"

"Why would he expect anybody to come nosing around this early?" Joe replied, thinking it more likely they'd find the police at the auditorium. Then Frank would have to give up this bizarre plan. "Frank, do you remember seeing the truck yet?"

"Not yet," Frank admitted. He sank back in his seat and put his hand to the side of his head. Each beat of his pulse was sending a little jab of pain through his skull. It seemed to get worse when he tried to concentrate. "But it'll come."

Up ahead, he saw the dark bulk of the Bayport Auditorium against the slowly brightening sky. The street in front was deserted. A police barricade blocking the parking lot entrance was the only sign of the disaster the night before.

Joe stopped down the block and looked back at Frank. "Do you think the cops have the place staked out?" he asked.

"I doubt it," Frank replied. "The terrorist target was the crowd, not the building. Why would they come back?" He pressed the bridge of his nose with his thumb and forefinger. "The police will be back later to go over the site in daylight. But for now I bet we'll have the place to ourselves."

Joe got out and shifted the barrier, then drove around to the back of the building and parked next to the hole made by the bomb, now covered with sheets of plywood. While Phil watched nervously, Joe used a crowbar to pry up one sheet.

Frank rummaged under the front seat of the van and produced three flashlights, then went in first. Joe and Phil quickly followed.

Inside, Frank paused. The lingering smell of explosives brought back a vague memory of groping in the dark, but that was all. He saw that the computer equipment had been left in place, off to one side of the stage.

"All right, let's not fool around," Frank said. "Why did the power go out? Did someone flip switches at the circuit breaker panels or at the main, or was there some kind of timing device that did it? Joe, you look around for signs of a short. Phil and I will check out the circuit breakers and the main power source."

While Joe headed offstage, Frank and Phil made their way to the lighting booth at the back of the auditorium. It was reached by a narrow staircase off the lobby. It was unlocked, and when Frank switched on his flashlight, he saw a console with banks of switches, knobs, and dials neatly marked with removable labels.

"This must be the place," Frank said. He bent down and shone his light on the underside of the console. "It looks okay. Anyway, the power went off in two stages. First the stage equipment, then the lights—including the emergency lights, which seems impossible since each one has its own battery, but let's try to solve each problem one at a time."

"It sounds like the main was shut off, rather than individual breakers," Phil said. "Let's see. . . ." He spotted two thick power cables and followed them up and along the wall into their circuit breaker.

"Bingo!" he said when he spotted the large metal cabinet. Frank followed him over to inspect it. Everything was in order.

"We have to find the main," Phil said, and went down to the lobby and started opening doors. He got lucky on his second try and found all the electrical equipment in one closet.

Two metal cabinets were hung on the back

wall. At the top and center of each were the charred remains of two disk-shaped metallic objects dangling from wires running out of the boxes. There were wires connecting the two devices to a single twelve-volt battery resting on top of the box on the left.

"These were attached to the mains," said Frank, being careful not to touch them. "But what did they do, and how?"

Phil studied first one disk and then the other. "They couldn't be simpler, Frank," he said. "I did something like this in fifth grade."

A little miffed, Frank took a closer look. On the nearest gadget, he could make out some numbers and a small motor attached to the rear. "What are they, old clocks?" he demanded.

"That's it," Phil replied. "My guess is, whoever rigged them took off the hour hands, attached one lead to the minute hand and taped the other one at twelve o'clock."

"I get it," Frank said. "When the minute hand reached twelve, it closed the circuit and shorted out the power for the building. But why not use the hour hand?"

Phil paused to yawn, then said, "You could, but your timing would be a lot less precise. This way, both devices went off within less than a minute of each other."

Frank frowned in concentration. "That means

these had to be installed within an hour before the blackout," he said.

"Either installed or set to go," Phil added. "That's a clue, isn't it? The bomber had to be on the premises."

"It seems that way," Frank replied. "But how did the emergency lights go out?"

"I haven't checked yet, but my guess would be that someone unscrewed all the bulbs so that when the batteries switched on, the lights still wouldn't come on. That the terrorist could do a while before the rally," Phil explained.

"You think you can trace these, Phil?"

Phil shrugged. "Maybe. They seem to be unusual, well-made clocks, with fancy numbers on the faces. And, hey, I think I see a serial number on the back of this one." He scribbled the number in a notebook he took from his pocket.

"If you've seen enough, let's get out of here," Frank said when Phil finished. "This place gives me the creeps."

They collected Joe and ducked back out under the loosened plywood. "Let's nail the plywood back before we go," Frank said. He glanced over his shoulder. The sky glowed orange to the east, but to the west it was still gray.

While Joe and Phil put the plywood back, Frank walked over to inspect the damage to the van. Suddenly he heard the throb of a car engine from the direction of the street. Had Joe replaced the police barrier across the entrance? He was trying to remember when a car came screeching toward him, its headlights riveted on him. He shut his eyes and turned his head away from the glare.

"Frank," Joe called urgently.

The car screeched to a stop and the two front doors were flung open.

"Police, freeze!" a harsh voice shouted. "All of you, facedown on the ground—*now!*"

Chapter

6

FRANK LOWERED HIMSELF slowly and carefully to the ground and lay flat, his arms outstretched. Next to him, Joe and Phil had joined him and were doing the same.

"Hey, take it easy, Eddie," came a familiar voice. "Two of those kids are Frank and Joe Hardy, Fenton Hardy's kids. They're okay. I don't know what they're up to, but I guarantee you won't need that thirty-eight."

Frank turned his head and looked up at Officer Con Riley of the Bayport Police Department. "Can I—" he started to ask.

"Just stay where you are, Frank," Officer Riley said, interrupting him.

"Officer Riley, my brother suffered a serious head injury last night," Joe said.

"I'm sorry to hear it," Riley said. "In that case, he ought to be in the hospital instead of out here making life hard for the police. Eddie, let them get up but pat them down, just in case they took some souvenirs from in there."

"You don't have to do that, Officer Riley," Joe said, rising to his feet. "We're part of the Webster campaign staff, so we wanted to take a look around before all the evidence disappears. But we didn't touch anything."

"Great," Riley said huffily. "Well, this is not your ordinary crime scene. We got the FBI breathing down our necks. Chief Collig is not going to be happy when he hears about this."

"You could spare him the grief, Con," Frank pointed out, pushing himself to a standing position. "Don't tell him."

"Sorry, fellows," the police officer replied with a shrug. "When Eddie and I saw the barrier had been moved, we called it in. We didn't know what we'd find. It's going to be a circus here in about three minutes."

Frank looked toward the street. Officer Riley had underestimated his department's response time. Already two squad cars were skidding into the lot, their lights flashing.

Con Riley nodded toward the van. "Get in," he said. "We'll follow you down to the station."

As they walked to the van, Frank leaned over to Phil and muttered, "Don't worry, buddy. If they throw you in the slammer, the boys'll bust you out."

Phil gave him a look that would have made a plant wilt.

Joe drove to the police station and parked out front. Con Riley's patrol car slid in behind him, and Riley came around to Frank's window.

"Well, fellows, aren't you lucky!" he said. "The nice lady on the radio says you get to meet with Chief Collig right away. Seems some Fed named Diaz is not happy about you guys snooping around."

As they walked up the steps to the station, Frank said, "Officer Riley, would you mind if I call someone from the Webster campaign before we see the chief?"

"There's a pay phone," Riley said, pointing down the hallway. "It's your quarter."

Frank reached in his pocket. No change. "Do you have a quarter?" he asked Joe. "I'm going to call Davids. Maybe he can give us a hand." Joe handed his brother a coin, and Frank dialed. The phone rang four times before Davids picked up.

"Hi, Dr. Davids?" Frank said, when the campaign coordinator answered. "It's Frank Hardy. Sorry to call so early, but we're downtown at police headquarters. We were brought in because we went back to the auditorium to look around. Yeah, I know . . . sorry. But here's the good news. We found the shorting devices used to black out the hall. And our friend Phil says they must have been set less than an hour before they went off. Right ... okay, thanks."

"What'd he say, Frank?" asked Joe.

"He's going to call Webster to bring him up to date," Frank replied. "Then he'll come down here and see what he can do for us."

"See, Phil," said Joe, "this is going to work out all right."

"Yeah, sure." The color had returned to Phil's face, but he wasn't happy yet.

"Okay, fellows, let's go." Riley led the way to Collig's office.

After Con pushed open Chief Collig's door, Joe saw the chief sitting behind his desk with Agent Diaz next to him. Both looked steamed.

The FBI agent glared at Joe, Frank, and Phil, then turned to Ezra Collig. "Chief, you promised me a secure crime scene," he said coldly. "The next thing I know, all of Bayport will be walking through it. I say, lock these kids up to teach them a lesson."

Ezra Collig's face was half-hidden by piles of papers on the desk. He had gray hair and heavy jowls. He was staring down at his desk unhappily. It was obvious to Frank that he didn't like having someone from outside barge into his office and tell him how to run his department.

"Boys," he said, raising his head. "Mr. Diaz

53

has a point. We've got a group of lunatics on the loose, setting off bombs, shooting at people, and you keep turning up in the middle of the action. If I locked you up, you'd at least be safe."

"We're working for the Webster campaign, sir," Frank replied. "And we didn't go looking for trouble. It came to us. As for this morning, we didn't disturb a thing."

"I told you not to meddle in this case," Diaz said. "How do I know you haven't disturbed the evidence?"

Chief Collig picked up a pencil and began tapping it hard on the desk to quiet the FBI agent. "So what'd you find, Frank?" he asked, pointedly ignoring Diaz.

Collig listened intently as Frank and Phil told him about the timers in the main power source. Then he leaned back in his old leather chair. "Interesting, don't you think, Diaz?" he said with a small smile. "When did you say you were expecting your gadget man? Later this morning? Maybe he can confirm this. In the meantime, it looks like we've got our second solid lead."

Before Diaz could reply, Joe said, " 'Second lead,' Chief Collig? What was the first?"

"Chief, I don't think—" Diaz started to say.

Ignoring him again, Collig said, "We got a report from the coroner a couple of hours ago. One of the guards had his throat slit before he

54

was blown up. Somebody got him inside the building. What do you bet it was the same somebody who planted those gadgets Phil found? And who knows, maybe that same somebody set off the bomb and then drove away in that red pickup truck."

Joe said, "The truck that so far only Frank, Alex Davids, and I have seen."

"Uh-huh." Collig gave Diaz a malicious smile. "Which means—and please correct me if I'm wrong, Agent Diaz—that so far most of the leads we've got in this case have come from these boys. Maybe instead of locking them up, I ought to deputize them!"

Diaz stomped out of the office without another word. As the door slammed, Collig's phone rang. Still chuckling, he picked up the receiver, listened for a moment, and said, "Tell him to wait there. I'm sending them down."

Collig hung up, then selected one of the many files piled on his desk and opened it. After a moment, he glanced up in mock surprise and said, "You boys still here? Go on, beat it. I've got work to do."

"Yes, sir," Frank said with a smile.

At the bottom of the stairs, Alex Davids was waiting for them. He was wearing a bright green nylon warm-up suit and red running shoes.

"I was sure you'd be able to handle this,"

Alex said with a smile. "But I thought I'd come check on you just the same."

Frank introduced him to Phil. "Good work, Phil," said Davids. "I phoned Nathan right after I talked to Frank. He was impressed with you all. Of course, he was also concerned about your difficulty with the police. But he's ready to vouch for you if you get in a jam and need his help."

"Terrific," Joe said. "And speaking of jam, is anybody else hungry? Rosie's is right across the street."

"Great idea," said Davids. "Breakfast is on me."

Frank noticed that Phil acted hesitant. "Anything wrong?" he asked.

"I hate to be a party pooper," Phil said. "But I've got to go home and get ready for school. It's seven already, and I wasn't lucky enough to get sprung from classes to work on a political campaign like you guys."

"Let me treat you to a cab instead of breakfast, then," Alex volunteered. "I'll go call one."

He walked over to the pay phone in the corner. A few moments later he returned and said, "A radio cab will be out front in five minutes, Phil. Here, this should cover it."

Phil seemed embarrassed about taking the money. "Thanks," he said. "You guys go on and have your breakfast. I'll just wait here."

As Alex and the Hardys were stepping off the curb, Joe said, "Hey, look. There's Chet Morton, on his way into Rosie's."

Joe ran ahead to catch up to Chet. He was almost across the wide street when Frank noticed a white sports car pulling out of a parking spot down the block. Suddenly the car accelerated and came hurtling down the block.

"Joe," Frank shouted, cupping his hands to his mouth. *"Jump!"*

Chapter

7

JOE LEAPT and landed on his shoulder, doing a quick tuck and roll onto the sidewalk. It was only when he looked back that he realized the car must have swerved away from him right before he'd jumped. He drew in a sharp breath as Frank and Alex ran toward him and the sports car skidded to a stop, then backed up toward them.

"Look out!" Joe shouted. "Here he comes again!"

The white sports car was approaching slowly this time. When it reached them, the driver braked and leaned out the window on the passenger side.

Joe's eyes widened as he recognized Ramon Diaz of the FBI.

"What are you—crazy? Dashing out into a street like that?" the agent said to Joe, totally aggravated. "It's just lucky I managed to avoid you."

"It looked to me like you saw me," Joe replied, equally miffed.

"Now I know you're crazy," Diaz snapped. "I'm an FBI agent, not a contract killer." He shook his finger at Joe. "Keep that in mind. And stop playing games!"

With that he put the car in gear and zoomed forward.

From the doorway of Rosie's, Chet Morton said, "Joe, you *know* that guy? You ought to talk to him about his driving."

Joe sighed deeply. "I can't believe it, but I think that was Agent Diaz's way of issuing a warning. He seems to have decided we're in his way."

"The guy must be a nut case," Chet said, summing up all of their reactions.

"Don't worry," Alex said grimly. "His superiors will hear about this. Whether he was aiming for you or not, his conduct was disgraceful."

"Well, at least no one was hurt," Chet said. "How about joining me for breakfast?"

They went inside, and Chet led them to a booth. On the table already were a stack of pancakes, two eggs over easy, toast, bacon, orange juice, and a cup of coffee.

"Hey, how did you order already," Joe asked as he squeezed in next to Chet.

"Rosie knows when to expect me," Chet said.

"But how could she forget the steak and home fries?" Joe asked.

"She didn't," Chet said, grinning. "They'll be out soon."

Alex and Frank settled in on the bench opposite them, and Frank introduced Alex to Chet. "Alex is running Nathan Webster's campaign in this area," Frank added.

"That's a pretty exciting job these days," Chet commented. "Not to mention risky. But look on the bright side. This morning's paper says that after last night's bombing, your man's running neck and neck with Montaldo statewide."

Frank frowned thoughtfully. "Then the terrorists aren't getting what they want," he said. "Which is good—unless it drives them to do something even more desperate."

"I understand your concern," Alex said. "But all Nathan can do is ignore the threat and go on campaigning. He had to cancel his speech in New York City tonight, but he's going to try to give a live press conference later."

"Under very tight security, I hope," Joe commented.

"I get the idea that you guys are working on

this case. Let me know if you need any help after school," Chet volunteered.

"Thanks, Chet," Joe replied. "We will."

"Have you got anywhere?" Chet continued.

"We've uncovered a few things," Joe replied. "The power at the auditorium was cut using shorting devices, which were wired up not long before the rally began. The person who wired them probably then waited near the stage door for the lights to go off. Then he knifed the guard, slipped outside, and attached a bomb with a tilt-fuse to the doorknob. When the knob was turned, *boom!*"

"He must have figured that there'd be such a commotion that no one would notice him pulling away in his pickup truck," Frank speculated.

Alex stroked his chin and said, "And whether or not he knew you saw his truck, he certainly knows that Joe and I could identify it after our little encounter with him last night. So I don't think we'll be seeing that truck around anymore. But what was that about a guard being knifed?"

Joe quickly related what Chief Collig had told them, then said, "Who could have got to those circuit breakers an hour before the show?"

"The only people around were technicians and campaign staffers," Alex told him. "The techies were partly from Nathan's computer firm, partly from the central campaign staff, and partly from the university here. I'd guess there'd be about thirty of them in all."

Chet scooped one last forkful of pancakes into his mouth, looked at his watch, and said, "I'd better go. I don't want to miss my mom's homemade biscuits. I have to have breakfast at home before school." As Joe stood up to let him out, he added, "Oh, hey, I happened to tape the late news last night for my dad. There was a long segment on all the protesters at the rally. You want to look at it?"

"Hmm," Frank said. "It never occurred to me that the terrorists might actually have had the nerve to demonstrate outside the rally before trying to blow it up. Can you bring the tape by Webster headquarters after school?"

"You got it," Chet replied. "Later, guys."

Joe sat back down. "I say we start by making a list of possible suspects."

Frank nodded. "Okay—at the top of the list is some way-out environmental group. But we can't forget that one of Webster's corporate competitors might be using the environment issue as a cover. Anybody else?"

Alex set his coffee cup down and said, "We also can't ignore the fact that Nathan is a presidential candidate. He's running for the most highly visible office in the world. I'm not saying a political rival would stoop to terrorism, but an overzealous supporter of the opponent might."

"Do you have anybody specific in mind?" Joe asked.

Alex hesitated. "Not exactly," he finally said. "But I have heard rumors about Al Scipione, who's running Josephine Montaldo's campaign in this area—rumors of a strong Mob connection."

"Some people say that about Montaldo, too," Frank pointed out. "I think it's just ethnic stereotyping—the idea that anyone with an Italian name has Mob connections. In fact, you said the same thing a few weeks ago."

"So I did, Frank," Davids admitted. "But the rumors about Scipione have been very persistent."

Frank stood up. "Callie's put in time as a volunteer for Montaldo. I think I'll give her a call to ask her to drop by Montaldo headquarters to see what she can learn."

When Frank returned, he said, "That was close. Callie had just called the hospital. When she found out I wasn't there, she got really worried. I caught her just as she was about to dial Mom."

"What did she say about Montaldo?" Joe asked.

Frank rolled his eyes. "She said we must be pretty desperate to buy that old Mob stuff. But I did get her to agree to go by her campaign headquarters after school and poke around."

"You know, you were asking about the computer techies who had backstage access yesterday evening," Alex said. "It occurs to me that many of them are probably at the auditorium this morning, trying to salvage some of the hardware we installed."

"Great!" Joe said. "I say we go straight there and ask questions."

"Good idea," Alex said as he picked up the check. "I'd come with you, but I have a huge backlog of work. Come by the office later and bring me up to date, will you?"

Outside, Alex retrieved his car and drove away. Joe and Frank crossed the street to the van and took off for the auditorium. Joe parked next to a van from the Bayport University Computer Center. A little farther along, among half a dozen police cars, he spotted Diaz's white sports car.

Masons were already at work replacing the blown-out brick wall. Joe and Frank showed their Webster campaign passes to a police officer and walked inside. Two men and a woman were working at the bank of computers. In the wings a man holding a clear plastic bag stood deep in conversation with Ramon Diaz.

Joe felt his hands tighten into fists. He took two steps in Diaz's direction before Frank grabbed his arm.

"Let him be, Joe," Frank said in a quiet

64

voice. "The less we have to do with him, the more we'll be able to accomplish. Come on, let's go talk to the computer people."

They walked over to the computer bank. One of the men, who was about thirty-five, glanced up and said, "Hi."

"Hi," Frank replied. "Are you going to be able to salvage much of the hardware?"

The man shook his head. "It's a real mess," he said. "Luckily, all those laptops out in the auditorium were pretty securely fastened to the flip-up desks, so we should be able to save them. Who are you guys with?"

"We're Frank and Joe Hardy, with the Webster campaign," Joe said. "How about you?"

"I'm with SemLab, Webster's company. Bill Mall's the name. Sarah and Claude here are with the university. We collaborated on this fiasco."

Sarah and Claude glanced up and nodded. Claude was a big, burly guy with a full black beard. He was wearing a plaid flannel shirt and blue jeans. All he needed was a pair of high lace-up boots, Joe thought, and he could be cast as a lumberjack.

"Got this one disconnected," Claude said, obviously not interested in small talk. "I'll take it out to the van."

Sarah continued to work, bent over another machine. Her blond hair was cut short. Her sharp, angular features and small dark eyes made her look a little like a squirrel at work on a nut. Frank turned to her. "Do either of you remember seeing anyone lingering around before the show began? Someone in the lobby."

"We've already talked to the FBI," Sarah said. "Now if you'll excuse us, we've got work to do."

"Sorry, guys," Bill Mall said, "but we're snowed. And there were a lot of people working here last night. It wouldn't have been unusual for anyone to hang around the lobby. Lots of folks were running up and down to the lighting booth. We had some problems getting the system running."

Joe glanced over at Frank. They couldn't really force Bill and Sarah to talk. Over Frank's shoulder, Joe saw that the guy in the flannel shirt was coming back. He looked about as friendly as a pit bull with a sore paw.

Right then Joe was taken by surprise by a yawn so powerful that it almost dislocated his jaw.

Frank grinned at him. "Yeah, me, too," he said. "Maybe we should go home and bag a few z's before we fade altogether."

"Good idea," Joe said. He looked over at the three techies and said, "See you later."

The three didn't seem thrilled by the thought. Joe led the way to the van and took the wheel. Though there were still a few wet spots on the pavement from the rain the night before, it was turning out to be a beautiful, sunny day. Joe turned onto the parkway.

The big house where Joe and Frank lived with their parents and Aunt Gertrude wasn't far from downtown Bayport, but the parkway saved at least ten minutes over using the traffic-clogged local streets.

As their exit came up, Joe flipped the turn signal and eased into the far right lane, slowly applying the brakes.

The pedal sank all the way to the floor, and the car didn't slow at all.

"Hold on, Frank!" Joe shouted.

Frank braced his feet against the dashboard. "Downshift!" he shouted back.

Joe grabbed the gear lever and forced it to the lowest position. The automatic transmission gave a loud whine of protest. Joe pulled hard on the lever for the parking brake. That helped, too. But as Joe steered around the gentle curve in the exit ramp, he saw a solid line of slow-moving traffic on the street up ahead.

"I can't do it, Frank!" he shouted. "I can't stop in time!"

Chapter

8

"THE BRAKES ARE GONE!" Joe shouted. "Hold on!" Gripping the steering wheel so hard that it made his knuckles white, he swung the van to the right. The tires scraped the concrete barrier on the side of the road.

Frank clamped his hands around the grab bar over his door as the front bumper hit the concrete, too.

"Keep it up, Joe," he called. "We're slowing down."

Now the whole side of the van was in contact with the barrier. Sparks flew. All at once a jog in the concrete abutment made the rear of the van slide out. Frank shut his eyes and braced himself as the van spun around and slid backward across the ramp. Then the back bumper slammed into the barrier on the opposite side and the van came to a stop.

After a moment's silence, Frank said, "Whew! Good work, Joe. You okay?"

"I think so," Joe replied, getting out and walking around to the front of the vehicle. "I think the van's going to need work, though. Would you pull the hood latch, Frank?"

While Joe poked around under the hood, Frank used the cellular phone to call their garage.

Joe came around to the window on Frank's side. "Just as I thought," he said, holding up a hand covered with reddish brown liquid. "There's no brake fluid left in the master cylinder. And the compression fitting to the brake line is loose enough to cause a slow leak. I don't think it loosened itself."

"Huh. I wonder if our auto insurance covers sabotage," Frank replied.

A car coming off the parkway slowed almost to a stop before edging past the disabled van.

Frank said, "I called Marty. He's coming with the tow truck, but maybe you'd better go up the road a little and flag people down. We don't want anybody to get hurt plowing into us."

The cellular phone beeped. Frank grabbed it. "Oh, hi, Mom. No, we're both fine. Why? Oh— Marty called the house? No, no, we didn't wreck the van. Really. But do you think you could pick us up at the garage in about twenty minutes?"

Frank replaced the phone and took a deep breath. He and Joe would need all twenty minutes to dream up a plausible explanation for the accident that didn't involve ecoterrorists.

Once home Frank collapsed on his bed and fell asleep. When he woke up it was past noon. He threw some cold water on his face, dressed, and went downstairs. Aunt Gertrude had returned from her trip and was in the kitchen, rolling out pie dough.

"You're a fine one," she said tartly. "First you tangle with a bomb and land in the hospital, then you don't have the sense to stay there until you've recovered. All this carrying on can't be good for your health. Are you hungry? There's turkey salad in the refrigerator."

"Thanks." Frank made himself a sandwich and added a handful of potato chips to his plate before sitting at the kitchen table to eat. "Where's Joe?"

Aunt Gertrude snapped her fingers, remembering. "He asked me to tell you—he's gone to pick up that van of yours. He should be back any minute."

As if on cue, Frank heard a car pull into the driveway and stop. He finished his sandwich and went out on the porch. The van looked as if it had got into a fight with a *Tyrannosaurus rex* and lost.

Joe climbed out and joined Frank on the porch swing. "Afternoon, sleepyhead," he said. He jerked his thumb toward the van. "One hundred fifty bucks—five for brake fluid and one forty-five for labor. Marty said he had to bleed the whole system to get all the air bubbles out of the brake lines. But everything seems to be working. Any thoughts on who tried to kill us this morning?"

Frank looked out across the yard. "Well, first of all, the brakes were probably fiddled with while we were in the auditorium. So whoever did it was definitely after *us* and not Alex."

"What about Diaz?" Joe asked. "You think he'd pull something like this?"

Frank replied, "The guy's obviously a total jerk. But unless he's out of his skull, I can't see an FBI agent purposely hurting us."

"I guess so," Joe said reluctantly. "So, either it was someone who saw us inside the auditorium this morning, or someone who arrived while we were inside and recognized the van."

"Right," Frank said. "Which probably means that it was someone with a reason or excuse for being there."

"What about that guy from the university computer center," Joe asked, "the one who looked like a lumberjack. Claude, I think. He made an excuse to carry a computer out to the parking lot while we were onstage."

"He wasn't what you'd call friendly, either, was he?" Frank said. "Of course, that doesn't make him guilty."

"But it wouldn't hurt to pay him a visit—since we've got no other plans. Do you know how to find the computer center?"

As he stood up, Frank said, "Sure. I was there just a few weeks ago, setting up an E-mail account for the Webster campaign office. Their mainframe computer is the local hub for Intercomp, the big on-line networking system."

"Then what are we waiting for?" Joe demanded. "Let's roll!"

Bayport University was built on a hill at the edge of town. Frank directed Joe to a parking lot near a three-story structure with a piece of rusty abstract sculpture in the front courtyard.

The interior was modern and depressing. Concrete block walls were painted institutional green—the floors covered with gray linoleum. There was a bored-looking guard sitting at a desk near the entrance. He looked up and said, "Can I help you?"

"We're with the Webster campaign," Frank replied. "We're here to see Claude," he added, hoping there was only one Claude who worked at the computer center.

"Oh, you'll have to speak to Hollis," the guard replied. "Through that door, first office on the left."

Hollis was a woman of about forty with a face set in a permanent expression of resentment. When Frank and Joe entered her office, she continued to stare at her computer monitor for what seemed like forever. Then she glanced over and said, "Yes? What is it?"

Frank repeated his request to see Claude.

"If you mean Claude Madlin, he only works mornings," she snapped, and turned back to her computer.

Frank stayed where he was. After another minute, Hollis peeked at him again. "What now?" she demanded.

"There was a woman named Sarah helping us earlier this morning at the auditorium," Frank said. "Could we—"

"Sarah Spano," the woman spat out. "Room Twelve-oh-three."

"Thanks for your help," Frank called out as he and Joe started for the hallway. He was secretly sure that his cheerful tone would aggravate Hollis more than anything else.

"Boy, what a grouch," Joe remarked in an undertone.

"Boy, what a setup," Frank echoed as they walked past a large room separated from the hall by a glass wall. Inside the room was what looked like the set for the main deck of the starship *Enterprise*. A bank of computers dominated the center of the room, and around the walls were tape decks, line printers, and terminals. Frank didn't see a single human in the room. Did the mainframe run itself?

Frank and Joe stopped at the open door of Room 1203. Joe tapped on the door frame. Sarah Spano didn't look up. She was sitting in front of a desktop workstation with a screen covered by a complicated network of multicolored lines.

Finally she turned to them, her face expressionless. "You were at the auditorium this morning," she said. She stood up and wandered over to a filing cabinet.

Frank smiled, even though she was keeping her back to them and wouldn't see. "That's right. I'm Frank Hardy, and this is my brother, Joe. We're with the Webster campaign staff. As you can imagine, our people are doing everything we can to help the FBI with its investigation."

Joe took over. "We were wondering if you remembered anything else that happened in the hour before Webster's speech started last night. Anything that might have struck you as odd."

Sarah turned around, clutching a file folder to her chest as if it were armor. "Like I told you before, I can't think of a thing," she said breathlessly. "We were all working under incredible pressure. None of us had ever done anything quite like that before."

"Was Claude Madlin with you during the whole hour?" Frank asked.

"I have no idea," Sarah replied, staring down at the floor. "There were a lot of people up there, at least thirty, and I only knew the ones from here. I didn't stand around taking notes on where everyone went. Why are you asking me about Claude, anyway?"

"We're asking questions about everyone," Joe said.

"Well, I don't have time to answer them." Sarah returned to her workstation and added, "Please leave me alone. I've got work to do."

So that's that, thought Frank as he and Joe left the office. Sarah was obviously stonewalling. But why? Did she have something to hide? Or did she simply not like their looks?

On the way out of the building, they stopped by the office of the secretary. Just as before, she took her time noticing them. Once she did, Frank said, "The Webster campaign needs a list of the people from the computer center who were working at the rally last night. Mr. Webster would like to thank them all and make sure they're okay."

Hollis glared at him for a moment, then muttered, "First Payroll wants the list, then the FBI, and now it's politicians."

She thumbed through the files on her desk, took out a sheet of paper, and photocopied it. "Here," she said, handing it over. "Anything else?"

"That's it, thanks," Frank said as jauntily as before. "Have a nice day."

Half an hour later Joe parked the battered van in front of the storefront building the Webster campaign had rented. As he and Frank got out, it began to drizzle.

Inside, a veteran campaign worker named Mike Conway spotted them and called out, "Hey, Frank, your girlfriend just called, from the Montaldo office. She said she'd try again later."

"Thanks, Mike," Frank said.

"That was good thinking, putting a spy in the enemy camp," Mike continued. "It's like the old days back in Brooklyn."

Frank interrupted him. "Did Callie tell you she was spying on the Montaldo campaign?"

Mike shrugged. "Not in so many words. But I'm a man who knows what two plus two makes."

"This time you added wrong," Frank said. "It's not what you think."

"Sure, Frank, sure," Mike said with a conspiratorial grin.

From the door to his office, Alex Davids called, "Joe? Frank? Do you have a minute?"

When the Hardys joined him, he added, "Your friend, Chet, just dropped by with that video. We were about to take a look at it."

Inside the office, a man and woman in business suits were standing near the television set. "Frank and Joe Hardy, meet Dana Forster and Judy Bloomfield," Alex said.

"The brains behind the campaign?" Frank said. "This is a pleasure!"

Forster coughed. "The brains behind this campaign belong to Nat Webster," he said. "But we do what we can to help. Alex has been telling us about you guys. It's nice to meet you."

Alex picked up the remote and pressed the Play button. On the screen Frank saw a shot of the front of the auditorium and lines of picketers. A few seconds later Alex gasped and hit the Pause button.

"You see that guy?" he said, pointing to a man holding a sign that read Save Mother Earth—Bury Webster. "I know him! It's Jerry Vespey. Back in the sixties we called him Jerry the Red. He was a leader of Students for a Democratic Society, and I heard rumors that he joined the radical underground near the end of the Vietnam War."

"You think he's one of the terrorists?" Frank asked, studying the grainy image.

"It's not impossible," Alex replied. "He lives nearby, in a commune called Green Fields. I know because they have a stand every Saturday at the Bayport Greenmarket. I've chatted with him a few times. He calls himself an ecopacifist these days and says that he's completely sworn off violence."

"Not that he'd announce it if he changed his mind," Joe pointed out. He picked up the control and hit the Play button again.

As they watched, Frank told Alex and the others about their investigation so far. Alex was very upset about the sabotage to the van and seemed inclined to tell the Hardys to drop the case. When Frank made it clear that they would go on whether the campaign backed them or not, he said, "Well, the least we can do is pick up the tab for the damage to your car. Send me the bill and I'll see it's taken care of."

"Thanks," Frank said. "Oh—here's a list of the people from the computer center who were working at the rally last night. You might pass it around. See if anyone spots a name that sets off bells and whistles."

"Hey, Frank," Joe called, pointing to a frame he had frozen. "Look at this."

On the screen was a close-up of a beautiful girl of about sixteen, wearing faded denim overalls and a purple T-shirt. She was carrying a sign that said Pull the Plug on Webster.

"I see what you mean," Frank said. "The terrorists told the newspaper they were going to 'unplug' Webster. That is suspicious."

Joe gave a sheepish grin. "Actually, I didn't notice the sign," he admitted. "I just thought the girl was a babe."

Before anyone could react to this, Mike came to the door and said, "Frank, there's a call for you on four from Vanessa. She says it's urgent."

"You can take it in here," Alex said, passing Frank the receiver and pushing one of the buttons.

"Hello?" Frank said, his heart sinking. "Vanessa? What is it? What's wrong?"

"I'm at Callie's house," Vanessa replied. "You'd better get over here right away."

Frank gripped the receiver tighter. "Why? Did something happen to Callie?"

"Yes! Scipione found out she was spying on him and decided to teach her a lesson." Vanessa's voice broke. "She's really scared, Frank, and so am I."

Chapter

9

FRANK TOOK A DEEP BREATH. Trying hard to keep the panic out of his voice, he said, "Don't worry, Vanessa. We'll be right there."

He hung up and spoke to Joe. "We have to go," he said in a low voice. "Scipione found out about Callie and put a scare into her."

"How—" Joe began, but stopped when Frank tilted his head in the direction of the doorway. Mike was standing there, watching.

Joe's expression tightened as he realized what Frank meant. He nodded sharply. "Right," he said. "Let's roll. 'Bye," he called to the others, and asked Alex to follow him out into the hall.

Frank exchanged a few quick words with the man. Then he and Joe hurried out. As they drove away, Joe said, "So Scipione's got a spy in the Webster campaign."

"It looks that way," Frank replied. "And whoever it is must have heard Mike talking about Callie, then passed the word on to his boss."

"You mean Scipione?"

"I don't know," Frank said. "But what if Callie found evidence that Scipione was involved in the bombing? What if the so-called Green Warriors are actually a front for the Mob?"

"And the guy in the red truck is really a hit man?" Joe suggested. "It's possible."

"If they've done anything to Callie . . ."

As they pulled up in front of Callie's house, Frank saw that her father was pacing up and down on the front porch. A distinguished-looking man with a shock of silver hair, he stopped and waited for Frank and Joe.

"Callie's had a pretty rough experience," he said. "It looks as if you fellows have got involved in a game of hardball this time."

"Sir, we—" Frank began.

Mr. Shaw held up his hand. "Frank, Joe—you know I have the greatest respect for you and your detective talents," he said. "But I think you may be getting in over your heads. Why don't you put this aside for a few days, just until your father comes home?"

"We'll think about it, sir," Frank promised.

"But the primary's tomorrow, and anything could happen between now and then."

Frank and Joe went into the house. Callie was in the living room, sitting on the couch. She looked very pale. When she saw Frank, she jumped up and ran over to hug him tightly.

"Oh, Frank, it was so awful!" she gasped. "I didn't know if I'd ever see you again."

"Here, sit down," Frank said, gently guiding her back to the sofa. At that moment Vanessa came into the room with two cups of tea. She handed one to Callie, who took a sip, then set the cup on the coffee table.

"Do you feel like telling us what happened?" Frank asked, taking Callie's hand.

She swallowed, then nodded. "I went to the Montaldo office right after school," she said. "They put me to work stuffing envelopes. That's all I did, that and keep my ears open. Oh, and I called Webster headquarters and left a message for you with a Mike Conway. I guess that was a mistake, wasn't it?"

"It seems like it," Frank replied, his jaw set. "Mike figured you were spying on Montaldo and told me so out loud. Everybody in the office must have heard him."

"And any of them could have called up Scipione to pass the word along," Joe added.

"One of them must have," Callie said. "Anyway, there I was, working away, when Scipione came over and said he wanted to see me in his office. I thought, Great, a chance to find out more about him."

Frank noticed that his fists were clenched. He took a deep breath and tried to relax. "It looks like you found out more than you wanted to," he said.

"I found out that the guy's a real creep," Callie said. "But not much else, I'm afraid. The minute I was inside his office, he started saying in this quiet, oily voice that nosy kids have to be taught a lesson. I knew I was in trouble right then, but tried to play innocent. And he mentioned you, Frank. He knew your name, and Joe's, and that you're friends with Professor Davids."

"It sounds as though his spy inside the Webster campaign is good," Frank commented. "What happened next?"

"It got *really* scary," Callie said. She fell silent and started to tremble. Frank put his arm around her shoulders.

"I'm okay," Callie said, giving a little shake. "Scipione must have pushed an alarm button or something, because the back door to his office opened and these two huge goons came in. They didn't say a word, just grabbed me and carried me out the back to a stretch limo. One of them threw me in the backseat and got in after me. The other one drove. I was too frightened to keep close track of where they took me, but I know it was over on the south side. Finally they drove the limo right inside some kind of old factory or warehouse and stopped."

Vanessa looked at her wide-eyed.

"Then the hood in the back forced me out of the car," Callie went on. "I saw that they'd parked just a few yards from a huge black furnace. Maybe it was an incinerator, I don't know. I could hear the roar inside it even before the other goon opened the fire door. And when I saw the flames, I started screaming as loud as I could, but I couldn't even hear myself over the noise. The guy who was holding me started pushing me toward it. I kicked and scratched and even tried to bite him, but he was too strong for me."

"You mean they tried to throw you into the furnace?" Joe exclaimed. "Unbelievable!"

Callie shook her head. "It turned out to be an act. They got me close enough for me to feel the heat on my face, then they just shoved me to the ground and drove off. I'll never forget the smiles on their faces. They smiled then like they'd done the funniest thing ever."

"When I catch up with them, it'll be the *last* thing they do in years," Frank growled. "What happened then?"

"I was afraid they'd come back to finish the job, so I hid behind some packing crates for a while," Callie said. "Finally I worked up the nerve to hike out to the road to find a pay phone."

"She called me, and I drove over to pick her up," Vanessa said. "Then I phoned you the minute we got here."

"What about the police?" Joe asked. "Did you call them, too?"

"No," Callie answered. "Dad wanted to, but we convinced him that you guys should hear about it first. And, anyway, what could the police do? Arrest those hoods for harassing me? It'd be my word against theirs *and* Scipione's. I wouldn't be surprised if they ended up pinning the blame on me and the Webster campaign."

At that moment Frank was very close to blowing his top. The thought of Scipione and his hired muscle treating Callie that way made him boil. He knew he wouldn't be much help if he didn't keep a lid on his anger, though.

"You were right not to go to the police, Callie," he said slowly and deliberately. "I think we'd better handle this quietly. If Scipione is behind the bombing, he'll probably make another move soon. After what happened last night and this morning, he must be getting desperate."

"This morning?" Vanessa repeated. "What happened this morning?"

"Someone played a nasty trick on us," Joe

explained. "He fiddled with the brakes of the van while we were parked at the auditorium. They went out on us when we started to get off the parkway. It was just good luck that we didn't end up being flattened."

"Good luck, and some really great driving by Joe," Frank added.

"I don't understand," Vanessa said. "You think Scipione's hit man sabotaged your brakes? But what was he doing at the auditorium, and how did he know the van was yours?"

"He knew the van from last night," Joe replied. "As for why he was there, maybe he simply came by to gloat over the damage he'd caused."

"But if Scipione went after Callie like that, he could know something about all of us," Vanessa pointed out.

"If he has a spy at Webster headquarters, there isn't much about us he doesn't know," Frank told her.

"Including the fact that you and Joe are investigating the case," said Callie.

"But no one could have known that before today," Frank commented.

"My head's spinning, Frank," said Callie. "I don't really see how all this fits together. Montaldo had a comfortable lead before this happened. Why would Scipione think he had to *kill*

Webster and terrorize so many people? It's too bizarre."

"I'd better bring Alex up to date on all this," Frank said. "May I use the phone?"

He stepped out into the hall. A minute or so later he returned. "Alex is out," he reported. "But Jan, his secretary, thinks he sent me an E-mail message a few minutes ago. Callie, I'd like to use your computer to check my mailbox."

"Sure," Callie replied. "Vanessa, I think I'll make another pot of tea. There should be some cookies in the kitchen, too."

"Sit still," Vanessa told her. "Joe and I'll take care of it."

"Come on, I'm not in such bad shape that I can't boil water," Callie responded.

Frank left them to settle the question. He went into the study, powered up Callie's computer, and gave it the command to dial the university mainframe. Once connected, he entered his ID and password, then typed MAIL. There were six files, including two from a criminology news group that looked very interesting. He logged them, just to be sure that they didn't get lost, then moved the cursor to the file from "adavids@bayuvm" and pressed F2 to bring it onto the screen.

The message was short. Nathan Webster was feeling better and would be giving a short press conference that evening at his hotel. Alex was on his way over there.

Frank pressed F5 and typed a reply in which he told Alex what had happened to Callie, warned him that Scipione had placed a spy at Webster headquarters, and explained that he and Joe were going to concentrate on Scipione. Then he pressed F5 once more to send the E-mail to Alex's box, and logged off.

As he went to rejoin the others, Frank thought of Scipione's hoods dragging Callie toward the fiery furnace. His nails were digging into the palms of his hands. He stopped and took several deep breaths, trying to reach the state of watchful harmony taught in martial arts. It worked—a little. But not enough.

"Here, have some tea and a cookie," Vanessa said when he walked into the living room.

"Thanks, I'm not hungry," Frank said. "Listen, about Scipione—if we all work together, we can keep his office under round-the-clock surveillance. With the primary tomorrow, he's got to make his move now or forget the whole thing."

Joe was standing near the fireplace. He looked at Frank with a puzzled frown. "Hold on, Frank," he said. "What do they say about putting all your eggs in one basket? Scipione isn't our only suspect, after all. We can't spend all our time and energy on him just because he put a scare into Callie. Anyway, he doesn't sound like anything more than a sleazy punk to me."

Frank stared at him, feeling his chest constrict. "Are you kidding?" he shot back. "It's obvious that Scipione is trying to scare us off because he knows we're onto him."

Vanessa said, "Hey, how about taking it easy? We're on the same side, remember?"

Frank started pacing like a caged animal.

"Besides," Joe added, "no matter how much of a slimeball Scipione may be, we've still got to check out Jerry Vespey. And I think we ought to take a very close look at his commune, too."

Frank boiled over. "Come off it, Joe," he snarled. "How can you brush aside what happened to Callie? You just want an excuse to go to that commune to chase after some New Age airhead. Did I let you down when Iola got killed?"

The moment the words were out of his mouth, Frank was ashamed. Iola Morton, Joe's girlfriend, had been killed by a bomb that was meant for the Hardys. It had taken Joe a long time to get over it.

"Iola?" Joe snapped. "What's Iola got to do with this? Are you saying that I'm not interested in Callie's safety or in solving this case?"

Frank felt that he had gone too far to back

down. "That's exactly what I'm saying," he said. "Look at the way you made a fool of yourself in front of Alex Davids and two of the most important people on Webster's staff—all because of some girl who caught your eye!"

Joe's face turned bright red, and his neck seemed to swell up. He stared straight into Frank's eyes for a long moment. Then, with no warning at all, he lunged forward and threw a hard left straight at Frank's stomach.

Chapter

10

THE FORCE OF JOE'S PUNCH sent Frank reeling. He crashed into a table covered with china figurines, and everything went flying. Stunned, he lay on the floor for a moment. Joe stood fuming over him.

"Joe!" Callie cried as she moved between them. "What are you doing?" Her voice was strained with emotion, but she stood rocklike, facing Joe down.

Without saying a word, Joe stomped out of the room. Vanessa went after him as Mr. and Mrs. Shaw ran into the room.

"What on earth!" Mrs. Shaw cried as she eyed the remains of her figurines scattered over the floor. "Have you all gone mad?"

Frank stood up, not knowing what to say. He picked up the overturned table and bent down to retrieve the broken china. "I'm sorry, Mrs. Shaw," he muttered. "Joe is . . ."

He broke off, realizing that Joe was not the problem.

"Look, Frank," Mr. Shaw said. "No one can blame you for being upset, but enough is enough. It's time to hand this case over to the authorities."

"Dad's right," Callie added, putting her hand on Frank's shoulder.

"But don't you see?" Frank said. "We'd be doing exactly what Scipione wants if we give in now. The police don't have any evidence against him. They'd drop the case. It's up to us to get it."

Frank looked over to the front hall as Vanessa came back. "Joe's taken off in the van," she said, panting. "He says he's going to Green Fields to investigate. I couldn't stop him. You know how he is when he gets an idea in his head."

Frank glowered at her. "I wish he hadn't taken the van," he said. He stopped speaking when he noticed the expression on Vanessa's face. "Are you okay?" he asked.

"Oh, sure, Frank," she answered. "Of course I am. My boyfriend's just run after some other girl, in a van that looks like it's been in a demolition derby, after knocking down his brother who was on the critical list just a few hours ago. And Callie was almost tossed into an incinerator by a couple of hoodlums. Sure, Frank, I'm terrific. No problem." She bit her lip, obviously trying to fight back her tears.

Frank put his arm around her shoulders. "Don't worry, Vanessa," he said. "Joe can get a little wild sometimes, but there's nobody more loyal. I shouldn't have said what I did about that girl. I guess I'm still shook up by everything that's happened today."

"We all are," Callie said. "I'll sweep up what's left of those toby mugs, then I move we take our minds off this by helping Dad make supper."

"Great idea," Frank said. "But first I'd like to let Alex know about Joe taking off like that."

Frank returned to the computer and discovered that there was another message from Alex in his box.

Frank,
    Joe called, wanting the location of Green Fields. He has some harebrained scheme to infiltrate the place in the guise of an agronomy student. I tried to talk him out of it, but no go. Are you in on this, too? I hope not. I thought you had more sense. Call or E-mail me soon.

                                                        Alex

Frank pressed his fingers against his eyelids. His head was starting to ache again. But he couldn't let himself give in to it. He sat up and wrote a quick reply. Once it was on its way through cyberspace, he headed for the kitchen. Callie and her dad were in a hot debate with Vanessa over whether onions should be chopped by hand or in the food processor.

"Excuse me, people," Frank said. "Any chance I can borrow someone's car for the night?"

"Sure, Frank," Vanessa said. "You can have mine."

"But you can't go until you've had some spaghetti, Frank," Callie insisted.

"Well, okay," he said.

Mr. Shaw slapped him on the back. "Good. That means I'll have a chance to try talking you out of pursuing this case."

When Joe called Alex Davids on the phone in the van, he was surprised to learn that the commune was near the Red Creek Nuclear Reactor.

Just before six, he noticed a gas station and convenience store and pulled in. The refrigerator case held a few plastic-wrapped sandwiches and cans of soda. He settled on ham and cheese and a cherry cola.

As he settled himself behind the wheel again,

he thought, Let's see, Joe—so far today you've had less than three hours of sleep, been arrested, almost been run over by an FBI agent, crashed the van, and slugged your brother, who nearly died the night before. Great work. Keep it up.

What he needed to do now was figure out how to get into the commune. Posing as a student interested in alternative forms of agriculture was a brilliant stroke, but could he pull it off?

No, he decided. It would probably be best not to pretend to know anything about farming, but just to act as if he had a strong interest in the subject.

The sun was setting when he spotted a weathered wooden sign that said Green Fields Farm, with a dirt road just beyond it. But he didn't turn off the highway. A quarter of a mile farther along he spotted a barely visible trail through a grove of trees. He cut the headlights, turned off the road, and drove down the trail until the van was totally out of sight.

As he walked back toward the entrance to the commune, he planned how he was going to explain his appearance and the fact that he'd arrived on foot. Then he noticed something odd about the place. "No telephone poles or power lines," he said under his breath. "What do you know—this place is already 'unplugged'!"

A slight rise and a line of trees shielded Green Fields from the highway. Once past them, Joe saw a cluster of wooden buildings that managed to look both old-fashioned and futuristic at once. Gardens and fields surrounded them. A windmill stood silhouetted against the evening sky, its blades slowly turning in the breeze. In the lush grass close at hand a volleyball game was just breaking up.

A man of about fifty with long gray hair, a beard, and a deeply lined face came toward Joe. "Jerry the Red himself," Joe muttered under his breath.

"Hello there," the man said cheerfully. "What brings you here—car trouble?"

"No," Joe said. "Actually, I hitchhiked here on purpose. I would have called, but you don't seem to have a phone."

"And what a blessing that is," the man said. "But what brings you to us?"

"I'm Brad Locke," Joe said, pulling a name out of thin air. "I'm doing a report for school, and I heard you know a lot about alternative farming techniques. So I wondered if I could interview you."

The man scratched his beard, then said, "It's a little late for that today. We go to bed with the sun and rise with it, too. But I'll tell you what—why don't you stick around till tomorrow? We'll put you up and then show you around. You won't have much luck hitchhiking back to town at this time of night, anyway."

"That's good of you," Joe said. "Thanks a lot."

The man held out his hand. "By the way, my name's Jerry Vespey. I'm one of the commune's elders. Come along and join us in our evening circle."

A bell rang, and Joe could see older men and women along with kids of all ages coming out of the main building to join the volleyball players. They all began walking over to a large campfire on the north side of the field.

As Joe followed Vespey, he studied the others. They all seemed normal enough, if a bit rustic in their bib overalls and sturdy boots. But their quiet, almost solemn march to the fire made Joe think of a primitive religious ritual.

When everyone had settled down on the benches arranged in a circle around the fire, Vespey stood and spoke. "Friends, we have a visitor tonight named Brad Locke. Please welcome him and help him feel at one with the spirit of the land."

Vespey pulled Joe up and gently pushed him toward a man extending his hand. While the group sang a song, Joe was passed around the circle by commune members who greeted him, clapped him on the back, and even embraced him. Their warmth astonished him. And when he found himself being pecked on the cheek by the gorgeous girl he had seen in Chet's video, he blushed to the roots of his hair.

Unfortunately, she quickly passed him along to a skinny old man who gave him a big bear hug.

Frank parked Vanessa's snappy little sports car across the street from the Montaldo campaign office and sat watching the comings and goings. With the primary scheduled for the next day, the joint was jumping. After about ten minutes, Frank decided on a more direct approach. He got out of the car, crossed the street, and entered.

He walked confidently through the front room, nodding to some of the people manning the telephones. At the back two big guys were standing next to a closed door. Frank was pretty sure they were the goons who'd given Callie such a hard time.

Hoping his stony expression would hide his disgust, he walked over to the one on the left and said, "Tell your boss that Frank Hardy wants to talk to him. I'm with the Webster campaign."

The thug eyed him slowly before going through the doorway. A few seconds later he returned. "The boss'll see you," he announced.

Frank walked in. A short, balding, overweight

man was sitting behind a desk that was too big for the room. "What can I do for you?" he asked.

Frank gave Scipione a hard look. "That was quite a stunt you pulled this afternoon on your worker, Callie Shaw," he said. "When the press finds out, it won't help Montaldo's chances one bit."

"I'm afraid I don't understand, Mr. Hardy," Scipione said smoothly. "The last time I had the privilege of meeting with Ms. Shaw, who is a Webster campaign worker, not one of ours, I made sure she was given door-to-door service home."

"Gee, boss," said one of the goons. "You think maybe I took her to the wrong door?"

The other thug snorted.

"Jimmy, we're going to have to work on your sense of direction," Scipione said.

Frank had had enough. He reached out to sweep the papers off Scipione's cluttered desk, but his hand came in contact with Scipione's black appointment book. "Well, well," he said, snatching it up. "I wonder if there's anything in here that might interest the press."

"Jimmy, Sal!" Scipione yelled.

Frank thought again of Callie's being menaced by these thugs, and his blood boiled. Without thinking, he leapt over the desk, wrapped an arm around Scipione's neck, and picked up a letter opener. "Any closer and I'll use this on your boss," he threatened. "Now, open the rear door and go outside, both of you."

"Go ahead. Do what he says," Scipione gasped.

Frank took a deep breath and got ready to shove his hostage out the door after them, slam it shut, and make a run for the front of the building.

Just then all the lights went out. An instant later Scipione's elbow hit him hard in the pit of the stomach. Gasping for breath, he let Scipione go.

"Now!" Scipione shouted. "Get him!"

Chapter

11

IN THE SUDDEN DARKNESS Frank shoved Scipione away, but the heavyset man was quicker than Frank expected. He felt a hand clamp down on his arm and start to spin him around. Not waiting for the next move, Frank delivered a karate kick straight ahead into the darkness.

"*Argh!*" Scipione cried. "He's over here, you idiots!"

Frank dropped to his hands and knees and crawled under the desk, then scuttled across the room. Just when he was sure he must be near the door to the main room he touched the toe of a shoe, which launched a kick straight at his head. Frank went into a quick roll, reached up to clasp the ankle, and yanked. One of Scipione's men was down. He landed heavily on the floor beside Frank.

Frank lunged forward, found the doorknob, and jerked the door open. In the darkened main room, the campaign workers were stumbling around, shouting questions to one another. Frank was threading his way toward the pale rectangle of the front door when he heard a gunshot. Over the screams of the volunteers, Scipione shouted, "Stop that guy!"

"He's over by the copy machine!" Frank shouted, and made a dash for the door. Once outside in the pale moonlight, he bent over double and scurried across the street to Vanessa's car, then jerked the door open, dove in, and tugged the door closed behind him, extinguishing the interior light.

As he drove away, Frank saw in the rearview mirror headlights in the alley that ran beside the office. He didn't wait to see if they belonged to a stretch limo. He didn't slow down until he felt sure no one was on his tail.

That was when the amazing fact finally sank in. The whole of Bayport was dark. No streetlights, no lights in houses—even the signals were out.

Frank glanced at his watch. It was a few minutes after eight. "Of course," he said to himself. "The blackout must have been timed to interrupt Webster's press conference. The Green Warriors strike again!"

He turned on the radio. His favorite Bayport rock station was off the air. He twisted the knob and found an all-news station out of New York City. According to their reports, power had been knocked out to the entire Bayport region because two important high-tension links had been damaged.

"We have learned," the announcer said, "that the Green Warriors informed the *New York Post* earlier today that they were prepared to strike again if presidential candidate Nathan Webster did not drop out of the race immediately. They have now warned that a major catastrophe will follow if Webster doesn't announce his withdrawal in the next twelve hours. Reached at the site of his disrupted news conference, Webster vowed not to give in to terrorist threats.

"Meanwhile," the report continued, "the agencies investigating last night's blast have reported little or no progress in the case...."

Frank suddenly recalled Scipione's black book. He had tossed it on the seat of the car when he got in. He pulled off onto a quiet side street, turned on the interior lights, and reached for it.

As he flipped through the pages, he saw that at least half of the entries concerned betting.

Scipione obviously liked the horses, but Frank couldn't tell if he was an illegal bookie or simply an avid gambler. There was one item that caught Frank's attention. It said, "PO shipment to incinerator," and a few days after, "Paid, PO $5,000."

He turned a few more pages and found another curious entry: "Meeting w/Acme Building Supply, re: PO," and a simple "PO—6 AM" jotted down at the top of the Election Day calendar square.

Callie had described the place she'd been taken as a warehouse. Could it have anything to do with "Acme Building Supply"? And did "PO" stand for power outage?

Still, there was nothing to suggest that Scipione had it in for Webster—no mention of bombs or the Webster rally.

Was Scipione a big-time crook, or just a small-time operator?

If Joe were here, we'd be able to talk it out, Frank thought regretfully. He was feeling tired and confused. He wasn't going to give up on Scipione just yet, but he was getting the distinct feeling that he was going in the wrong direction. Maybe Joe wasn't off-base after all. In that case, Frank had let his brother rush into a possibly dangerous situation at Green Fields Farm—with no backup.

Frank rubbed his temples and tried to plan a

strategy. Maybe he should stake out Montaldo headquarters early the next morning to see what, if anything, happened at six A.M. After that, he could go by the university to try to catch Claude Madlin. And if *that* didn't lead anywhere, he would get directions from Alex and drive out to Green Fields to check on Joe, if Joe hadn't returned home.

But right now what he needed most was sleep. He wasn't thinking straight, he knew. And his head was pounding.

Joe woke the next morning to the sound of a clanging farm bell and the sweet, fresh smells of a dew-covered farm. He was on a feather bed in a small room that smelled like cedar paneling. A chipper young voice broke through the haze in his head with the happy news of buckwheat pancakes on the griddle.

"Hurry up, Brad," the voice called. "They'll all be gone if you don't get up soon."

A smile crossed his face as he recognized the voice. It belonged to the beautiful girl he had first seen in Chet's video. She was Vespey's daughter, he had learned, and her name was Rosebud. After the campfire the night before, she had promised to show him around the commune.

Joe sprang out of bed, pulled on his clothes, and dragged his fingers through his hair, then hurried downstairs to the big dining hall. Everyone else was already seated at the long table, apparently waiting for him. Rosebud smiled and pointed to an empty chair between her and her father. Feeling his cheeks grow warm from all the attention, Joe circled the table and sat down.

The bell rang again. A smiling woman in her fifties stood up and said, "Let us give thanks to Gaia, mother and provider." She raised a glass of water, took a sip, passed it to the person next to her, and then continued, "Gaia gives and takes. She nurtures with rain and chastens with thunder, and in the end we all return to her."

Everyone was silent while the glass went around the table. When it reached Joe he took a sip, too.

Once the glass returned to the woman who had spoken, she sat down. The hum of conversation and the rattle of dishes filled the room.

Joe took two pancakes from a plate that was passed to him, slathered them with butter and maple syrup, then turned to Rosebud. "Who is Gaia?" he asked.

Her alert gray eyes peered deep into his. "Gaia is a name for Mother Earth," she explained. "We see the whole planet and everything on it as a single system that nourishes life. That's why it's so important to cherish and protect it."

"I see," Joe said with a nod. He looked

around and added, "Am I right that the walls are made of old tires?"

On his other side, Vespey smiled. "Quite right," he said. "It's something I learned from an old friend in New Mexico. Fill old tires with dirt, stack them up, and you get a simple, strong, cheap, and very well-insulated structure."

"This room is so warm in winter," Rosebud added, "that we don't always have to use the wood stove."

"And every tire we use is one less tire clogging the country's landfills," Vespey said. He returned to his breakfast. So did Joe. The buckwheat pancakes were delicious, and the maple syrup tasted one hundred percent pure.

The people around the table drifted out as they finished eating. After breakfast, Joe found himself standing near one of the big windows with Vespey and Rosebud.

"I noticed there aren't any power lines out here," he said. "But I saw lights on last night. Is that electricity all from the windmill?"

"Partly," Vespey answered. "But we use so little electricity that the solar panels on the roof usually handle our needs. The windmill is a backup for short winter days and long periods of overcast skies."

"It sounds like you're going both backward and forward in time," Joe said, fascinated by the blend of old and new technologies.

"We're not escapists," Vespey said seriously. "We're trying to come up with a viable lifestyle for the future." He paused a second to reflect. "Nobody out here wants to spend much time on gadgets, though. We're mostly farmers. I've got a buddy in town who comes out and fiddles with the stuff."

Interesting, thought Joe. He was tempted to ask if the buddy happened to drive a red truck. But that would be the end of the Brad Locke pose. He decided to play a different card.

"You know," Joe said, "what you say about using technologies to prepare for the future sounds like what Nathan Webster has been saying."

"Not even close," said Vespey, sounding annoyed. "Webster's ideas about the future are hopelessly out of date, like some science-fiction movie from the sixties. He still believes that if you unleash the scientists, everything will turn out fine. What we're saying is that you've got to be selective about technology. We put the biosphere first. I don't believe Webster even considers it."

"I see what you mean. I guess I hadn't thought it all out." Joe gazed out the window. Was it time to push Vespey a little? "But you're just a handful of people. How can a small group like yours make a difference? People like Webster have an awful lot of money and power."

Vespey put a big hand on Joe's shoulder and said, "Sometimes a handful of people with good ideas can change the world."

Rosebud gave her father an adoring look, then said, "I promised to show Brad around, Dad. We'd better get started."

The sun was still low on the horizon and the dew glistened on the grass as they walked to the side of the main building, where a ladder leaned against the roof.

"Let's go up and get an overview of the farm," Rosebud said, starting to climb.

Joe followed. At the top, he almost lost his balance when he found himself face-to-face with a goat. The animal gave him the once-over, then went back to munching on the grass that covered the gently sloping roof.

"So even the roof is organic!" Joe exclaimed.

Rosebud smiled proudly. "That's right. It's energy efficient and self-maintaining—with a little help from Billy there. And we'll never have to replace it. No dumping truckloads of old roofing shingles into a landfill."

"Wow!" Joe said, genuinely impressed with the view. Everything nearby was green and flourishing. Farther away, beyond a band of trees, loomed a concrete structure that Joe recognized.

Rosebud noticed his glance and said, "When I come up here, I wish I could blow up that nuclear power plant. Everything would be so peaceful and beautiful if it weren't there."

Joe recalled that Callie felt the same way about the plant. But after all that had happened, it made him uneasy to hear Rosebud talk about blowing things up.

"Anyway, this is Green Fields," she said with a sweeping gesture. "We've left the outskirts of the farm alone to give wild creatures plenty of room. And, of course, a fourth of the land stays fallow every year."

A flash of light caught Joe's attention. He suddenly saw that his van was only partially hidden by the trees he had driven into. Would Rosebud spot it?

She didn't seem to notice. "Let's get shovels and I'll show you the composting operation," she said.

Joe followed her back down the ladder and around the main building to a shed, then helped her open the door. As his eyes adjusted to the dimness inside, he saw an old red pickup.

"I don't know why we keep this old wreck," Rosebud said. "It takes up so much room, and we never use it."

Joe glanced down. The tire marks in the dirt looked fresh. Disregarding Rosebud's curious glance, he stooped down and touched the exhaust pipe. It was warm.

Chapter

12

As Joe straightened up, Rosebud said, "Brad, what on earth are you doing?"

Joe smiled and replied, "I love old cars and trucks. Somebody's put a lot of work into this baby."

"I can't believe you, Brad!" Rosebud said teasingly. "Here I am, trying to show you how we've learned to work with nature, and all you care about is a machine."

"Well, boys will be boys," he said with a grin. He went to the passenger side, leaned in the window, and opened the glove compartment. Inside, wrapped in an oily rag, was a 9mm automatic. He quickly closed the compartment and glanced back at Rosebud. Her back was to him as she took down two shovels from a rack of tools.

She was smiling when she turned back to him, utterly sweet and trusting.

Suddenly Joe decided to take a very big chance—one he probably would never have taken had Frank been around. He needed help if he was going to crack this case before the terrorists struck again.

"Rosebud?" he said. "Listen, there's something I have to tell you. Can I trust you?"

She looked up at him. "Of course, Brad," she said. "What is it?"

Joe took a deep breath. "I'm not Brad Locke. My real name's Joe Hardy, and I came here because I'm on the track of the terrorists who bombed the Nathan Webster rally on Sunday. I know I've found them. But I'm betting my life that you're not one of them."

By 5:45 A.M. Frank was parked just down the block from the Montaldo campaign office. He had left Vanessa's sports car at home and borrowed his dad's nondescript sedan with tinted windows.

Workers had succeeded in getting the lights back on in Bayport, and Frank hoped it was a sign that things would go better.

Just before six, a U.S. Postal Service truck pulled up in front of the building. A uniformed letter carrier got out and went inside, then came out again with the two big thugs Frank had tangled with the night before. The three men started lugging sacks of mail from the mail truck to a black four-wheel-drive vehicle parked nearby. Then they dragged other bulging mail sacks from inside the office and put them in the postal service truck.

As the postal service truck drove away, Frank noted its license number, and decided that he had to find out what was in those sacks. He waited until Scipione's men went back into the building, then sneaked over to the black vehicle. The rear door was not locked. Holding his breath, he pulled it up and climbed inside, letting the door close behind him.

The clasps on the mail sacks were not locked. He flipped one open, loosened the drawcord, and reached inside. All the contents were the same: preprinted envelopes addressed to the Bayport Board of Elections. The words "Absentee Ballot" appeared in big letters on the front of each envelope.

The truth hit him like a ton of bricks. Scipione was planning to rig the election by substituting phony absentee ballots for real ones! He'd obviously bribed postal workers to sort out the real ballots, put them in sacks, and bring them to Montaldo headquarters. Fake ballots were now headed to the Board of Elections for tabulation. Frank knew that the voting would be close—maybe so close that the phony absentee votes would give Montaldo the lead.

Frank grabbed three of the real envelopes and stuffed them inside his shirt. He was starting to edge the door open when he heard someone just a foot or two away, say, "Okay, let's roll." Moments later the front doors opened and shut and the engine started. Frank waited, poised by the back door until the vehicle started to move. Then he thrust the door open, jumped to the pavement, and sprinted to his father's car. He expected to hear shouts or even gunshots, but apparently Scipione's thugs hadn't noticed.

Fifteen minutes later the envelopes were on Alex Davids's desk, and Alex was on the phone to the FBI. "That's right, I'm talking mail fraud and election-rigging," he was saying. He gave them the license numbers of the postal service truck and the black four-wheel-drive vehicle, and suggested that FBI agents make a fast trip to Acme Building Supply. "If you and the local police move fast enough, I bet you'll find all the evidence you need there—especially if you hang out at the incinerator," he concluded. "If you don't, Nathan Webster and every reporter in the country are going to want to know why."

He hung up and smiled at Frank. "That ought to light a fire under them," he said. "Good work, Frank. I should have remembered that

Scipione was the lawyer for some postal workers who were caught in a mail-dumping case. I guess he set up this scam through them."

"I'm glad we put a stop to it," Frank said.

"And maybe this little black book you brought me," Alex went on, tapping Scipione's diary, "will tell us who the Montaldo spy is in the Webster campaign."

"Right," Frank said, then paused. "But we still have no proof who did the bombing."

Alex opened his mouth to reply, then glanced over Frank's shoulder and remained silent. Frank looked around.

Nathan Webster was walking slowly toward them, with the help of a cane. His left arm was in a sling, and his hat only partly covered the white surgical tape that was wrapped around his head. He waved off his bodyguards and closed the office door behind him.

"Alex, Frank," he said. "I came in person because I wasn't sure the phone lines were secure. I looked over that list of people you sent me and recognized one of the names."

"You did?" Alex exclaimed. "Who?"

Webster sat down. "A man who worked for me in the days when I was first developing the microchip that put my company on the map. A good mind, but very erratic. Anyway, one day over coffee, I told him about a particular dead end I'd come to, and he made a remark that gave me the idea I needed to get around it."

Frank suddenly saw where the story was heading. "But this guy got it confused and decided it was his idea and that you'd stolen it from him, right?"

"Exactly," said Webster. "Poor Claude—he became rather unhinged, to the point that I finally had to let him go. The last I heard, he was working as a part-time computer technician. I didn't know that he was in this area, and I certainly didn't suspect that he was one of the people installing the system for Sunday's rally."

"The man you're talking about is Claude Madlin, isn't he?" Frank said. Webster nodded. "I bet he didn't have a heavy beard when you knew him. And on Sunday I'm sure he stayed out of your sight. He was my top suspect until I got onto Scipione." He explained why he and Joe had suspected Madlin of sabotaging their brakes.

"I think you'd better pursue this, Frank," Webster said. "I'd pass it on to the FBI, but I don't think they'd be interested. They seem to have decided that the campaign against me is the work of some German splinter group called the Green Fists.

"I'm sorry to say this about someone I used to know and like," he added. "But I'm afraid Madlin might be capable of almost anything."

*   *   *

Joe and Rosebud were sitting on the rail fence around the farm's sheepfold. He'd just told her all about the attacks on him, his brother, and the Webster campaign.

"You see," he concluded, "someone driving that red truck shot at me and Professor Davids. And it's a good bet that he knifed the guard and set off the bomb at the Webster rally, too. My brother saw the truck speeding away soon after the bomb went off."

Rosebud looked at him with wide eyes. "Brad!" she said. "I mean, Joe! So did I! We had a picket line in front of the auditorium. We were taking a break when we heard the explosion. And then I thought I saw the truck driving away, but there was a lot happening and I forgot about it."

Joe asked, "Was your dad with you when you saw the truck drive away?"

"Sure," she said without hesitating. "All of us were hanging out in front. We were planning to wait and picket at the end of the rally, too."

"Then who could have been driving the truck?" Joe asked her.

"I don't know, unless . . ." She fell silent, then burst out, "I never trusted that guy!"

"What guy?" Joe demanded.

"Somebody my dad's known a long time," Rosebud told him. "He comes out here to keep

the machines going. His name's Claude—
Claude Madlin."

Joe stared at her. "Does he work at the Bayport University Computer Center?"

She frowned. "Yes, I think so."

Joe jumped down from the fence. "He knows
my face and that I'm after him. Do you know
where he is now?"

Rosebud frowned. "Well, no. He shows up
here usually every day, though. He—"

Joe interrupted her. "I've got to get out of
here before he turns up today and spots me.
Listen, Rosebud—if you run into him, you'll
have to act like nothing has happened. Don't
let on that I was even out here. If your dad
asks, tell him I hitched back to town."

He jumped down from the fence, then looked
back at Rosebud. She was staring at him with
wide, frightened eyes. Joe suddenly understood
why. "Rosebud?" he said. "Are you afraid that
your dad is part of this thing?"

She gasped and put a hand to her throat. "I
don't know," she said. "He and Claude had a
big argument the other day. Claude didn't want
us to picket at the rally, but Dad insisted."

"Madlin was being smart," Joe said. "If you
hadn't gone, I wouldn't be here nosing around."

Rosebud shook her head. "I can't believe that
Dad knew what was going to happen, though.
He would have tried to stop it."

"Are you sure?" Joe asked gently. "Maybe he ran out of patience. . . ."

Rosebud sank to the ground and buried her face in her hands. Her shoulders shook. Joe sat down next to her and put his arm around her.

Then he remembered what Alex had said about Vespey joining the radical underground. "He ran out of patience once before, didn't he? During the Vietnam War."

She nodded and raised her head, her cheeks wet with tears. "I know," she said. "Mom told me about it before she died. But my dad never hurt anybody. He had a buddy who did bad stuff—"

"Like what?" Joe asked intently.

Rosebud started to sob softly. "I don't know, maybe something like planting a bomb. . . ."

"Did your mother say who his friend was?" Joe probed.

Rosebud shook her head.

"You realize," he said, "that it could have been Claude Madlin. I've got to get out of here and get help."

Rosebud went with him halfway to the grove of trees. As he said goodbye, she squeezed his hand and said, "Good luck. And—whatever happens, don't think badly of Dad. He's a good person."

Joe walked quickly to the van. As soon as he was clear of the commune, he would use the cellular phone to call Alex and the FBI. With the license plate number of the truck, they'd have no trouble intercepting Madlin when he left to carry out his next act of terrorism.

Joe got behind the wheel and turned the key. The engine started at once. He backed out of the woods, turned onto the highway, then reached for the phone. It was dead. He was slowing down to take a look at it when he felt something cold touch the back of his neck.

"It's temporarily out of order," someone said in a deep baritone. "Drive on."

Joe slowly lifted his eyes to the rearview mirror, afraid of what he'd see. A chill ran down his back. Claude Madlin was there holding an automatic pistol on Joe.

Chapter

13

"I HEAR you've taken up organic farming," Madlin said. He gave an odd chuckle and added, "Too bad your brother, Frank, doesn't share your interest. If he weren't off chasing some cheap gangster, the two of you could have been the latest recruits to the Green Warriors. But I guess I'll have to make do with just you."

Joe glanced at Madlin in the mirror again. the terrorist was sitting back now, but the blue-black automatic in his hand was still leveled at the back of Joe's head. What had he said about a "cheap gangster"? That had to be a reference to Scipione.

"How do you know what my brother's doing?" Joe asked.

Madlin chuckled again. "I've been reading his E-mail," he replied. "Oh, don't look shocked. E-mail is even less private than sending someone a postcard. Any competent hacker can get into it."

His tone changed. "Okay, when you reach Route Ten-A, turn left. And don't try anything, or I'll ice you as fast as I did that guard the other night."

Joe tried to control his breathing. Madlin had just admitted to cold-blooded murder. What chance was there that he would let Joe live to testify against him?

"Where exactly are we heading?" Joe asked.

"I like the way you said 'we,' Joseph," Madlin boomed. "It shows you're becoming a solid member of the group. *We* are dropping off some packages at three different power substations. Afterward we'll use a radio transmitter to set off a fireworks display, in honor of the presidential primary. But I'm afraid the people of New York City won't enjoy it when they discover they have no electricity."

Joe tried to imagine the chaos a prolonged blackout would bring to New York. After a few hours the emergency generators at the hospitals would stop, and the patients on life support would begin to die. The subways and traffic signals would stop working, creating total gridlock. Banks, television networks, stock exchanges—almost everything would shut down. Looters and muggers would rule the darkened streets. . . .

"Why is Jerry Vespey letting you go on with this crazy plot of yours?" Joe demanded.

For a long moment Madlin was silent. Joe risked another glance and saw the madness in the man's eyes. He felt doomed. "I've got that idiot right where I want him. I told him I'd implicate him in a little bombing affair I pulled off in the sixties. We were good buddies back then, and he believes I can make it stick," he continued, then laughed without a trace of humor.

The chill along Joe's spine deepened. Had Vespey known this morning that Madlin was planning to kidnap and probably kill Joe? Rosebud was so sure that her dad was a good guy, but even good guys can go crazy when scared.

Joe cleared his throat and said, "One thing I don't understand. After the bombing, why did you risk coming after Alex Davids and me?"

"I got angry," Madlin confessed. "The radio announced that Webster had survived. I knew security would be too tight around him to try again. I knew from their E-mail how close Webster and Davids are, so I decided to get at Webster through Davids. But I didn't count on your driving skill. That just made me madder. So I made a little adjustment to your van."

Joe's eyes finally met Madlin's in the rear-view mirror.

"You know, you make it sound as if Nathan Webster is a personal enemy of yours," he remarked.

Madlin sat up and jammed the gun barrel painfully deep into Joe's neck. "Enough talk," he growled. "Just drive."

While Webster alerted the FBI and the local authorities about Madlin, Frank and Alex drove to the campus computer center. The same secretary was at the same desk, and once again she waited a couple of minutes before acknowledging them.

"What is it?" she demanded.

"I'm Professor Davids, from the political science department," Alex said in a level voice. "Is Claude Madlin in?"

Hollis's tone changed. "Oh—I'm sorry, Professor, he left before I got in. I hope he's not ill."

"Maybe we should go check on him at home," Frank said. "What's his address?"

"We're not allowed to give out that information," she replied.

"Then I suppose I'll have to get it from the provost's office," Alex said. "May I use your phone?"

"Oh, that's okay," Hollis said, grinning up at

him. "I suppose I can give it to *you*." She scribbled something on a piece of paper and handed it to Alex, then glared at Frank.

Frank put on a big smile. As he and Alex were leaving, he turned back and winked.

Madlin's home turned out to be an aging garden apartment building two stories high, built around three sides of a sun-baked lot that once must have been a lawn. They found Madlin's stairway and went inside. His apartment was on the second floor. Frank rang the bell and waited, then rang again. Nothing. After a quick glance around, he took out a plastic credit card and tried to open the lock with it. No luck.

"I'm going to have to pick it," Frank murmured to Alex. "Keep an eye out."

Opening the lock involved positioning three separate picks in exactly the right places at the same time. After what seemed like forever, the lock clicked. Frank swung the door open slowly, paused, then ducked inside and gestured for Alex to follow.

It was a simple studio apartment. The efficiency kitchen was on the far side of an open archway. A wooden door resting on two file cabinets served as a desk, on top of which lay a powerful computer and stacks of books and papers. Frank was heading for it when Alex grabbed his arm.

"Look at that!" he exclaimed.

On the wall over the sofa was a big corkboard thick with newspaper clippings. One glance told Frank that they were all about Nathan Webster. "Here's one that goes back to 1968," Frank said as he scanned them. "And look—this is about the bombing, from yesterday's paper."

"He drew a smiley face on it," Alex remarked. "The man's obviously out of his mind."

Frank glanced down at his desk, and his eyes widened. "Alex! Look at this!" he shouted. "It's a printout of our E-mail messages from last night. He must have read them this morning when he got to work."

"So he knows that Joe went to Green Fields," Davids pointed out. "Do you suppose that's what made him leave in a hurry?"

Frank stared. "You mean because Joe *was* on the right track after all, and Madlin was afraid he'd stumble onto something out there?"

"Could be," Davids said. He scratched his chin. "On the other hand, Madlin may have simply left work to carry out his next act of terrorism. He *did* promise to do something very big."

Frank suddenly felt tired and helpless. "I'm going to call the FBI," he announced. "Now that we know Madlin's the man, they can handle it a lot better than we can."

The phone was on the wall just inside the kitchen. Frank was lifting it to dial when he noticed the sheet of phone numbers taped to the wall. Halfway down the list, he saw "Emerg # Gn Fields, call Paul Adams, 555-7248."

"Alex!" Frank shouted. "Madlin is connected with Green Fields! He's got an emergency phone number for them. That cinches it. Now I know that Joe's in trouble."

"Then we ought to get the FBI out there," Davids pointed out.

"If Madlin already has his hands on Joe, an FBI raid won't help," Frank replied. He closed his eyes and tried to think. There was only one answer. "I'm going out there."

"I'll come with you," Alex said. "I've been there before, so I know the way. And I'm the one who roped you boys into this in the first place."

They left quickly, after making sure nothing looked disturbed, and made good time getting out of town. Following Alex's directions, Frank turned north onto the highway.

"I was there just once, last fall," Alex reminisced. "They were celebrating the first of the maple syrup with a pancake breakfast open to all their friends. I had a great time. But Jerry can be a pretty tough character—politically, at least. As far as he's concerned, if you aren't one hundred percent with him, you're not with him at all."

Frank frowned. "Even so, how could a man like Madlin, who seems to be deranged, convince a whole group of pacifists to help carry out a vendetta against one man?" he wondered aloud.

"I think Madlin must be *using* Green Fields," Alex replied. "Either the members don't realize what he's up to, or there's some sort of coercion involved."

"You did say that Jerry Vespey may have joined the radical underground during the Vietnam War," Frank reminded him.

"That was then," Alex replied sharply. He didn't seem to want to continue the discussion, so Frank concentrated on his driving.

As the sign for the commune came into view, Frank asked, "Should we hide the car and go in on foot?"

"We don't have time," Alex said. "Just turn in, and we'll start by questioning anyone we see."

A little past the turnoff Frank noticed a woman in the field on the left, turning the last of the crop under. She was guiding an old wooden plough pulled by two sturdy horses. She saw them and waved.

"She looks friendly enough," Frank said, stopping the car.

"You talk to her," Alex replied. "I'll go on ahead and try to find Vespey."

"Whoa!" the woman called when she saw Frank walk across the furrows to her. She was a stout, handsome woman in her forties with light brown skin and dark hair.

She brushed a lock of the dark hair off her forehead and said, "What's the matter, friend? Lost?"

"Not exactly," Frank replied. He had decided to be as direct as possible. "I'm Frank Hardy from the Nathan Webster for President campaign, and I think there's a terrorist group operating out of your farm."

"Hoo, boy!" the woman said, rolling her eyes. "Some of us wondered if we'd get hassled for demonstrating at that rally."

Frank put all the earnestness he could into his voice. "Look, it's not like that," he said. "My brother came out here yesterday afternoon to investigate. He hasn't been heard from since, and I'm worried."

"You mean the blond guy Brad?" the woman asked. When Frank nodded, she said, "He seemed pretty nice, even if he is a Webster supporter. Rosebud took him off after breakfast for a tour of the farm. They should be back by now."

"Could you do me a favor and look for him?" Frank begged. "We're afraid that one of the terrorists, a man named Claude Madlin, may have come after him."

"Madlin?" The woman's face hardened. "Huh. I'll see what I can do."

129

She tied the horses' reins to a fence post. Then she and Frank walked across the field toward a big barn.

"Wait here," she said. "I'll see if anyone in the house knows anything."

Frank glanced around. Where had Alex gone? Was he questioning another commune member?

Suddenly he heard a muffled cry from inside the barn. He was starting in that direction when a man with long gray hair and a gray beard stepped through the doorway. The double-barreled shotgun in his hands was pointed straight at Frank.

"Inside, quick," he ordered. "And don't make a sound!"

Chapter

14

FRANK RECOGNIZED JERRY VESPEY from Chet's video. The exradical was breathing fast and appeared ready to snap.

"Inside," he repeated, gesturing with the barrel of the shotgun. "Now!"

"Hey, take it easy," Frank said, raising his hands to shoulder height. He walked into the barn and found himself in a ten-foot-wide aisle lined with wooden stalls.

"At the back. Move it!" Vespey said.

Frank walked to the last stall and looked inside. Alex was lying on the straw-covered floor, his arms flung wide. He wasn't moving.

Frank gasped and took a step backward. "Is he—" He couldn't finish the sentence.

"I knocked him out, that's all," Vespey said. He sounded regretful. "Lie down next to him. I'm going to tie you up."

Frank sank down onto his knees in the straw, then looked up over his shoulder. "You know this is the end of the line, Jerry," he said. "The FBI is already on your case. Make it easy on yourself, instead of harder."

"What do *you* know about it?" Vespey said as he tied Frank's hands behind his back.

"More than you do, I suspect," Frank replied. "Do you realize that Madlin is just using you for his private vendetta against his old boss, Nathan Webster? This isn't about the environment, it's about one unbalanced person's desire for revenge."

Vespey paced back and forth. "I know Claude Madlin a whole lot better than you do," he said tensely. "And I know what I have to do."

"Do you know he slit a security guard's throat on Sunday night?" Frank retorted. "Do you call that protecting the environment?"

Vespey's face contorted with anguish. "Of course not. And I didn't have anything to do with it."

Frank knew for sure now that the man was close to the breaking point.

"I didn't have anything to do with the bombing either," Vespey went on. "But when Claude showed up here today asking about the young guy who came to the commune last night, I had to go along with him. I had to let him go after the kid. Otherwise—"

At that moment a babble of voices rose from the front of the barn. Frank looked up. The woman he had spoken to earlier was walking up to Vespey, accompanied by the beautiful girl in the news video.

"Otherwise what?" Frank shouted.

"We know what's going on, Jerry," the woman said. "For the sake of the commune, it has to stop—now."

"Otherwise what?" Frank repeated.

Vespey slumped against the side of the barn and collapsed into himself. For a long moment he said nothing. Then he shook his head and looked up at the girl sadly.

"It's okay, Daddy," she said, touching his shoulder lightly. "Brad told me all about Claude. But I know *you* would never do anything wrong—not willingly, at least."

Vespey snorted. "Not willingly is right," he said at last. "But this morning Claude told me he planted the bomb at the rally and rigged a blackout in Bayport last night, and that he's planning something even more terrible for today. He wanted to know all about Brad. He said he was going to take care of him first, and that if I tried to stop him he'd—" Vespey's voice broke and his shoulders shook with sobs.

"What, Daddy?" the girl begged. "You can tell us. It's all right."

Vespey looked into her shining face, and it seemed to give him courage to go on. "He said he'd tell the police I helped him bomb a defense plant during the sixties. I didn't know it at the time, but he did it—and three people were killed! Apparently the cops never even suspected him. But Claude kept some letters I wrote him that make it sound as if I played a part."

The girl gasped. Vespey dropped the rifle and put his hands on her shoulders. "You've got to believe me. Both of you," he added, turning toward the older woman. "This commune means everything to me. I want to change the world, but not with gun and bombs."

"We *do* believe you," the woman said.

Frank nodded.

"I had to go along with him, Rosebud," Vespey said, his voice cracking. "Don't you see?"

Rosebud wrapped him in a hug, and he sighed deeply.

The woman came over and bent down to untie Frank and Alex.

"Did you find my brother?" Frank asked her.

"Claude must have him by now." Vespey said. "Once I told him about Brad Locke, or whatever his name is, he went crazy. He'd already spotted a strange van parked among the trees near the road."

Alex sat up and gingerly touched the back of his head. "Whoo," he said. "Jerry, if you treat all your friends and customers this way, you're going to be out of business before you know it."

Vespey, abashed, said, "Sorry, Alex. I got in a panic and lost my head."

"And nearly took mine off, by the way it feels," Alex grumbled.

"So when Joe drove off, Madlin must have followed him," Frank said, his heart sinking.

"Well, no," Vespey said. "Claude was planning to shift the explosives from his truck to the van and use that for the mission."

"What explosives? What mission?" Alex demanded.

"Madlin's planning to blow up the transformer substations that supply power to New York City." Vespey looked ashamed and defeated, his eyes on the ground.

"But when Joe found out the van wasn't there, he would have come back here!" Rosebud said, sounding near tears.

"Madlin must have ambushed him," Frank said. He felt as if he'd just taken a hard punch to the stomach. "Do you know where he's going?"

For an instant Vespey stared into the distance, as if considering the possibility of stone-walling. Then he nodded and said, "Yes. His first target is the substation about thirty miles north of here, right on the Sound, that knocks down the high-voltage current from the Red Creek Reactor. I'd take you there myself, but they'd be gone long before we got there."

Following Madlin's instructions, Joe turned off the highway onto a narrow asphalt road that led through dense woods in the direction of the Sound. After a mile or so the complex of trans-formers came into view. It took up approxi-mately a half an acre in the middle of a large clearing surrounded by a chain-link fence.

Joe had often seen these giant assemblages of wire, bulky metal boxes, and contact arms. But he had never thought much about what they actually did. Clearly, Madlin had.

Madlin ordered Joe to pull alongside the fence and stop the van. "Okay, now get out, nice and slow," Madlin said as he slipped up through the space between the two front seats. He was careful to keep the automatic leveled on Joe.

"Go to the back of the van, take out one of the boxes you'll find there, *very* carefully, and carry it over to the fence," Madlin went on.

Joe followed the orders precisely, with Madlin behind him every step of the way. Inside the back of the van there were three metal boxes, each a little less than a cubic foot. Next to them was a gadget that looked like a control box for a model plane. He took the box nearest him. It was heavy.

Once he had set it next to the fence, Madlin handed him a pair of wire cutters. "Get inside there," he said. When Joe hesitated, he added, "I can shoot you now if you prefer."

Joe took the snippers and cut a hole in the fence large enough for him to climb through.

Madlin smiled. "Good! The rest is easy." He threw Joe a set of handcuffs. "Put one of these bracelets around your wrist and the other on the handle to the box."

Joe did as he was told.

"Good," Madlin said once more. "Now take this pair and put one around your ankle."

Joe did so, all the while casting about desperately for a way to escape.

"How you do this is entirely up to you," Madlin said. "All you do is carry that box into the middle of the transformer grid, choose a transformer that appeals to you, and attach your ankle to one of the ladder rungs welded to the side. Any questions?"

Joe looked at the power substation, then back at Madlin. "Yeah," he said. "What happens then?"

Madlin gave him a crazed smile. "Don't

worry about that," he said. "You'll enjoy a peaceful morning here in the countryside. And when what happens happens, you won't feel a thing."

"We've got to get there before Madlin puts his plan in motion!" Frank exclaimed. "But how?"

One of the commune members stepped forward. "There's a small airport about five miles from here," he said. "Maybe someone could take you there in a helicopter. Meanwhile, we could radio a message to the authorities."

"I can fly a helicopter," Frank replied. "Are any of you marksmen?"

Vespey stepped forward. "I'm a good shot," he announced. "And there's a thirty-thirty in the house. I'd like a chance to help."

Frank stared at the man in disbelief.

"Let him do it, Frank," Alex said. "I think we can trust him."

"I know the people who run the airport, too. They transport some of the produce we raise," Vespey added.

Frank didn't like it, but he didn't have a handy alternative, nor enough time to think of one. "Get your gun," he told Vespey. "I'll get my car."

Minutes later they were speeding toward the highway. "They must just be getting there,"

Vespey said after a glance at his watch. "With luck, we can reach them before they move on to the next target."

The airport was right on the highway. Frank swung in and drove toward the only building.

"A lot of well-heeled types fly out here on weekends from the city," Vespey explained.

"We're in luck," he added. "There's Walter."

Frank came to a stop next to a lean, silver-haired man in a blue nylon jacket. He looked over with a questioning expression. Vespey jumped out.

"Walter," he said, "we've no time for small talk. We've got big trouble and we need help."

"Sure," Walter said, his eyebrows rising when he saw Vespey's rifle. "On second thought, what's this about?"

"Frank's brother has been kidnapped by the terrorist who set off a bomb at the Webster rally," Vespey told him. "The folks back at the commune contacted the FBI, but there's a time problem. We need a chopper. Frank can fly it."

"Can you handle a Bell Two-twelve?" Walter asked skeptically.

"Is the main bearing seal okay?" Frank retorted. "Some of them have developed leaks at really inconvenient times."

"Okay, Jerry, the kid checks out," Walter said. "And, yes, friend, the seal is just fine. I'll get the keys."

Less than five minutes later, Frank and Vespey were airborne. Frank set a course northward and started scanning the terrain for the substation. The Sound glistened in the sun beyond.

"There!" Vespey shouted over the din of the engine. He pointed ahead and to the left. "Take her down a little."

Frank leaned forward and peered at the ground. The equipment-cluttered clearing was right in front of him.

"I see the van!" he shouted, pushing the control stick farther forward to descend. "Somebody's walking toward it. I can't tell if it's Joe."

Vespey checked over his rifle, jacked a shell into the breech, and looked out again. "Wait a minute," he said. "There's someone in the middle of the substation. He's not moving. It looks like he's tied up!"

Joe was on the ground next to a transformer with his ankle attached to it and his wrist attached to the heavy metal box. He knew his situation was hopeless, but when he heard the chopper overhead, he began to hope anyway.

Madlin was running toward the van. There was a *whap* from above, followed by the sound of a bullet ricocheting off the van. The people in the helicopter were shooting at Madlin! Whoever they were, that made them the good guys in Joe's eyes.

Madlin suddenly turned and started running back toward Joe. What's he doing, Joe wondered. There's no cover here.

Then, as Madlin kept coming, Joe realized that *he* was the cover Madlin was after.

The terrorist dove on top of Joe, then rolled him over and pointed the 9mm at his temple. The gunfire from overhead stopped.

"All they have to do is wait you out, Madlin," Joe said as the chopper withdrew a hundred yards or so. "Why not give it up?"

"Because I hold the trump card," Madlin said, panting. "There's a backup timer on each of the bombs. One substation is better than none."

"But it'll blow both of us up, too!" Joe shouted in desperation.

"Let it," Madlin replied. "What do I care?"

Chapter

15

DESPERATE, JOE TENSED to make a last attempt at overpowering his lunatic captor. He was ready to risk being shot by Madlin. That might be an easier way to go than waiting to get blown up. Then the noise of the helicopter grew louder. He looked up.

The chopper was going into a dive directly at him and Madlin. Joe was sure Frank was at the controls. This maneuver wasn't in any of the FBI- or police-training manuals.

Still crouched behind Joe, Madlin watched in silence. Then, as the chopper loomed larger, he raised his pistol and aimed it. Joe reached up with his free hand, grabbed Madlin's arm, and yanked with all his strength.

"Argh!" Madlin gasped as he went flying over Joe's shoulder. He landed on his back in front of Joe. The gun sailed gracefully through the air and landed in a shower of sparks on one of the electrical devices. After a moment of lying inert, Madlin pulled himself to his feet and ran limping toward the hole in the fence. Joe was still chained to the bomb.

Up above, Frank pulled hard on the controls. Centrifugal force pushed him back against the seat cushion as the chopper leveled off. He saw Madlin running for the van.

"Turn it around, Frank," Vespey yelled. "I can't draw a bead from this angle."

"No, I'm taking her down," Frank replied. "I'm going to cut him off."

No time for a neat floating touchdown, Frank thought. He did the best he could with what amounted to a controlled crash. He veered over toward the van, skimming just over Madlin's head, and set the helicopter down with a hard thump.

In that same instant Frank slapped the quick release on his shoulder harness. As he jumped out, he shouted to Vespey, "Don't shoot! We want him alive!"

Frank hit the ground running and dashed toward Madlin. He easily gained on his stunned quarry. As soon as he was within reach, he launched himself in a flying tackle, hitting the backs of Madlin's knees with his shoulder and wrapping his arms around Madlin's legs. Madlin came down with a thud but immediately got up onto his knees and started crawling.

"Hold it right there, Claude," Jerry Vespey said. He was standing in front of Madlin, pointing the 30-30 at him. "It's over now."

"Turning coat, Jerry?" Madlin said.

"I'm just doing what I should have done this morning," Vespey replied.

Suddenly Madlin lunged for the gun and pushed the barrel down into the ground. "Fool!" he cried. Vespey tried to yank it out of Madlin's grip but he was no match for the larger man. He fell backward when Madlin got to his feet and pulled the barrel up into the air.

Frank ran up from behind Madlin and tried to grab the rifle, but Madlin swung the gun and slammed the butt into his kidneys. Frank gasped with pain and fell to the ground.

As Madlin turned the rifle to point it at Frank, Vespey jumped between them and grabbed the gun by the barrel and stock. For a minute he and Madlin wrestled for the weapon. Then there was a muffled bang. Vespey took a step back. Madlin sank to his knees, and fell face forward to the ground.

Frank looked out across the clearing to where Joe was still trapped. He ducked through the hole in the fence and started to run toward him.

Then he saw that Joe was cupping his hands to his mouth. Frank stopped and heard, "The key—get the key!"

When he turned back, he saw Vespey digging into Madlin's pocket. Jerry tossed Frank a ring of keys, and Frank raced to free Joe.

"Pretty good flying, guy," Joe said as Frank unlocked the two sets of handcuffs.

"Thanks," Frank said. He gestured toward the metal box. "That's a bomb, right? Why don't we get out of here before it decides to go boom!"

"We've got some leeway," Joe replied. "Madlin still had two other bombs to put in place, and he was planning to set them all off at the same time."

"Just in case, why don't we take them all over to the edge of the clearing, then get out of here?" Frank urged.

"Good thought," Joe agreed. "And once we're well out of range, we can set them off with the remote control unit. It's hard on the nerves to have unexploded bombs lying around."

After shifting the bombs, Frank and Joe went over to where Vespey was still standing over Madlin's body. Madlin's eyes were closed, and blood was running from his abdomen into a dark puddle on the grass beside him.

Frank bent down to feel his pulse, then shook

his head. "He's dead, Jerry." He stood and gently patted the older man on his back. "You really saved the day here. And I won't forget it."

Vespey nodded but then said, "I never wanted to kill him."

"I know," Frank replied quietly. "And so will everyone once I give my statement. I'm not sure how the law will look on what happened this morning between you and Madlin, but my dad knows a few good lawyers who can help. Madlin forced you to keep silent about his plans."

The two of them climbed into the van. A minute later, Joe joined them. He was holding the remote detonator. "I don't know what the range is on this gizmo," he said.

"We don't know the power of those bombs, either," Frank pointed out. "Why don't we—"

He broke off as a gray sedan with a flashing red light on its dashboard came speeding into the clearing. On the trail behind it was a whole caravan of cars and emergency vehicles.

"Company, Joe," Frank said.

A loudspeaker blared. "You in the car, this is the police! Come out with your hands up!"

"I thought we already did this bit," Joe muttered as he, Frank, and Vespey climbed out of the van. "Why do they always show up just in time to miss the fun part?"

Agent Diaz walked around the back of his car

and came toward them, his .38 Special pointed straight at them.

"I don't think you'll need that, sir," Joe said. "Madlin's dead."

Frank added, "But if you brought along ear-muffs, maybe you'd like to stick around and watch us set off Madlin's bombs."

Diaz allowed a thin smile to cross his face. Then he scowled. "Do you have a federal permit to mount a fireworks display?" he demanded.

Joe was on the point of losing his temper when it occurred to him that Diaz was joking.

"No, sir," he said. "We couldn't afford the licensing fee."

Diaz laughed, holstered his pistol, and walked over with his hand extended. "Good work, you two," he said. "Unorthodox but effective. Congratulations. But—would you mind if we leave those bombs to the bomb squad?"

As Diaz radioed a report back to his base, Joe saw a black sheriff's car snaking its way past the line of vehicles. When it stopped, Nathan Webster and Alex Davids got out.

"Boys," Webster said, "I came as soon as I heard what was happening. I wasn't sure I'd see either of you alive again. After all you've done, you deserve cabinet seats."

"I hear that early exit polls are showing Nathan with a twelve percentage point lead," Alex said, grinning broadly. "So he may even be able to make good on that promise."

Frank laughed, but Joe seemed to be taking the suggestion seriously.

"Thank you, Mr. Webster," he said at last. "I wish I could say that I'm going to vote for you today when we get back. But I have to tell you that I won't. I just can't."

Webster raised his eyebrows, obviously taken aback. "Well, Joe, that's up to you, of course," he said. "But would you mind telling me why not?"

"It's nothing personal, Mr. Webster," Joe answered with a mischievous grin. "It's just that I'm too young to vote."

Frank and Joe's next case:

Frank and Joe's new classmate, Lindsey Nichols, is more than drop-dead gorgeous—she's pure trouble. An expert motorcyclist, she loves to take risks, and wherever she goes, danger is sure to follow. Her father's company is putting a classic bike back on the market, and the plan has led to a high-stakes corporate dispute. When the Hardys take sides, they also find they've taken their lives in their hands. Someone's out to kill the new bike before it hits the market—and killing may be the only way to do it. Dodging firebombs, bullets, and muscle-bound, chain-wielding bikers, Frank and Joe vow to down the saboteur before the fight spins out of control ... in *Wild Wheels*, Case #104 in The Hardy Boys Casefiles™.

THE HARDY BOYS CASEFILES